Italy's Contemporary Politics

I0655821

In early 2020 Italy was a country whose political parties stood as significant obstacles in the way of resolution of its social and economic problems. The purpose of this book is to help the reader to understand how Italian politics had reached this point. It does this by tracing the most significant processes of political, economic and social change to have marked Italian history in recent years back to their roots in the Italian political system as it emerged at the end of the Second World War. Starting with the restoration of democracy, the volume discusses the post-war party system and how it came under increasing pressure from the mid-1970s. From there it discusses the political upheavals of the early 1990s and the transformations they led to, the rise and fall of Silvio Berlusconi, and the watershed election of 2018. In short, the book provides a narrative. Narratives tell us who we are, where we have come from, where we are now and where we are going. Without them, we cannot make sense of the world. At the end of this narrative, if it has done its job properly, Italian politics and current affairs should 'make sense' if before they seemed confusing.

James L. Newell is former Professor of Politics at the University of Salford. His recent books include *Corruption in Contemporary Politics: A New Travel Guide* (2018) and *Silvio Berlusconi: A Study in Failure* (2019) (both published by Manchester University Press) and the edited volume *Europe and the Left: Resisting the Populist Tide* (Palgrave Macmillan, forthcoming). He is founder and co-editor of the quarterly journal *Contemporary Italian Politics*.

Europa Introduction to...

The Focus titles in this series build on the unparalleled worldwide coverage of The Europa World Year Book and its associated regional surveys: Africa South of the Sahara; Central and South-Eastern Europe; Eastern Europe, Russia and Central Asia; The Far East and Australasia; The Middle East and North Africa; South America, Central America and the Caribbean; South Asia; The USA and Canada; and Western Europe, also available online at www.europaworld.com. Books in the series provide students, postgraduates, academics, professionals and researchers with up-to-date, balanced, authoritative and concise introductions to topics in the Europa core areas of country-specific contemporary politics and economics, and regional and international affairs. Volumes in the series, authored by experts, present a factual overview in a concise format, offering readers the opportunity rapidly to research current issues.

Italy's Contemporary Politics
James L. Newell

Italy's Contemporary Politics

James L. Newell

Routledge
Taylor & Francis Group

LONDON AND NEW YORK

First published 2021
by Routledge
2 Park Square, Milton Park, Abingdon, Oxon OX14 4RN

and by Routledge
605 Third Avenue, New York, NY 10017

First issued in paperback 2022

Routledge is an imprint of the Taylor & Francis Group, an informa business

Publisher's Note
The publisher has gone to great lengths to ensure the quality of this reprint but points out that some imperfections in the original copies may be apparent.

British Library Cataloguing in Publication Data
A catalogue record for this book is available from the British Library

Library of Congress Cataloging-in-Publication Data
Names: Newell, James, author. | Routledge (Firm)
Title: Italy's contemporary politics / James L. Newell.
Description: First Edition. | New York : Routledge, 2020. | Series: Europa introduction to– | Includes index.
Identifiers: LCCN 2020027090 (print) | LCCN 2020027091 (ebook) | ISBN 9780367471323 (Hardback) | ISBN 9781003041900 (eBook)
Subjects: LCSH: Italy–Politics and government–2018-
Classification: LCC JN5453 .N48 2020 (print) | LCC JN5453 (ebook) | DDC 320.945–dc23
LC record available at https://lccn.loc.gov/2020027090
LC ebook record available at https://lccn.loc.gov/2020027091

ISBN: 978-1-03-239986-7 (pbk)
ISBN: 978-0-367-47132-3 (hbk)
ISBN: 978-1-003-04190-0 (ebk)

DOI: 10.4324/9781003041900

Typeset in Times New Roman
by Taylor & Francis Books

Contents

Tables

Preface

My aim in writing this book has been to make Italian politics since the Second World War comprehensible to the interested outsider. The way I have chosen to go about this is by telling a story: a story that begins with the dismissal and arrest of Benito Mussolini on 25 July 1943, and ends with the return home of a 24-year-old aid worker, Silvia Romano, on 10 May 2020, nearly 77 years later. The reason I have chosen to go about the task in this way is that to tell a story is to present a narrative. Narratives tell us who we are, where we have come from, where we are now and where we are going; and whether we are aware of it or not, we live in, through and by narratives. They are what make social life meaningful. So, my invitation is to read the book as if it were a novel. If I have carried out my task successfully, then by the end of the book the reader should have achieved understanding. That is, Italian politics should be comprehensible in the sense that the reader is able to appreciate both the underlying mechanisms and causal links connecting the event with which we start and the one with which we end, as well as the reasons for the actions of the principal protagonists of the story.

Narratives inevitably reflect the biases of their creators in terms of what they include and what they leave out. The present one is no exception, and because of space limitations it could not have been otherwise. If having read this text the reader decides to delve into the subject matter in greater depth, then historical figures, institutions and processes which could have been but are not mentioned in the text can be explored first by considering the texts mentioned in the guide to further reading at the end of the final chapter and then by consulting the lists of references in those books.

I decided to write this book at the invitation of Routledge's Europa Commissioning Editor, Cathy Hartley. The writing of the book was made practically possible thanks to periods as a visiting scholar at the universities of Torino, Urbino and Luiss Guido Carli between 2019 and the beginning of 2020. Franca Roncarolo, Luigi Ceccarini and Lorenzo De Sio were responsible for securing these visiting periods for me. To all three of these people I owe a debt of gratitude. I also owe a debt of gratitude to Alison Phillips for her painstaking work in copy-editing the manuscript. The result is a real improvement over the original. The responsibility for any errors in the text remains with me alone.

James L. Newell
June 2020

Abbreviations

AN	Alleanza Nazionale (National Alliance)
AP	Alernativa Popolare (Popular Alternative)
BR	Brigate Rosse (Red Brigades)
CAF	Craxi-Andreotti-Forlani agreement
CGIL	Confederazione Generale Italiana del Lavoro (Italian General Confederation of Labour)
CISL	Confederazione Italiana Sindacati Lavoratori (Italian Confederation of Workers' Trade Unions)
CLN	Comitato di Liberazione Nazionale (Committee for National Liberation)
CCD	Centro Cristiano Democratico (Christian Democratic Centre)
CD	Centro Democratico (Democratic Centre)
CI	Civici e Innovatori
CP	Civica Popolare
CpE	Centristi per l'Europa (Centrists for Europe)
DC	Democrazia Cristiana (Christian Democrats)
Demo. S	Democrazia Solidale (Solidary Democracy)
DL	Democrazia è Libertà (Democracy is Freedom)
DP	Democrazia Proletaria (Proletarian Democracy)
DS	Democratici di Sinistra (Democrats of the Left)
ECSC	European Coal and Steel Community
EEC	European Economic Community
EMU	Economic and Monetary Union
ENI	Ente Nazionale Idrocarburi (National Hydrocarbon Corporation)
EU	European Union
FdI	Fratelli d'Italia (Brothers of Italy)
FI	Forza Italia (Forward Italy, or Come on Italy!)

FLI	Futuro e Libertà per l'Italia (Future and Freedom for Italy)
GDP	Gross domestic product
GS	Grande Sud
IdV	Italia dei Valori (Italy of Values)
IMF	International Monetary Fund
IMU	Imposta Municipale Unica (Single Council Tax)
IRI	Istituto per la Ricostruzione Industriale (Institute for Industrial Reconstruction)
IV	Italia Viva
LeU	Liberi e Uguali (Free and Equal)
LN	Lega Nord (Northern League)
M5S	MoVimento 5 Stelle (Five Star Movement)
MAIE	Movimento Associativo Italiani all'Estero (Associative Movement Italians Abroad)
MDP	Articolo UNO—Movimento Democratico e Progressista (Democratic and Progressive Movement)
MSI	Movimento Sociale Italiano (Italian Social Movement)
NATO	North Atlantic Treaty Organization
NCD	Nuovo Centro Destra (New Centre Right)
NCI	Noi con l'Italia
NGO	Non-governmental organization
NPL	Non-performing loan
OECD	Organisation for Economic Co-operation and Development
P2	Propaganda Due masonic lodge
PaP	Potere al Popolo (Power to the People)
PCI	Partito Comunista Italiano (Italian Communist Party)
PD	Partito Democratico (Democratic Party)
PdCI	Partito dei Comunisti Italiani (Party of Italian Communists)
PdL	Popolo della Libertà (People of Freedom)
PDS	Partito Democratico della Sinistra (Democratic Party of the Left)
PLI	Partito Liberale Italiano (Italian Liberal Party)
PPI	Partito Popolare Italiano (Italian People's Party)
PpI	Popolari per l'Italia
PR	Proportional representation
PRC	Partito della Rifondazione Comunista (Communist Refoundation Party)
PRI	Partito Repubblicano Italiano (Italian Republican Party)

PSDI	Partito Socialista Democratico Italiano (Italian Social Democratic Party)
PSLI	Partito Socialista dei Lavoratori Italiani (Italian Socialist Workers' Party)
PSI	Partito Socialista Italiano (Italian Socialist Party)
RAI	Radiotelevisione Italiana (Italian Radio and Television)
RI	Rinnovamento Italiano (Italian Renewal)
RC	Rivoluzione Civica (Civil Revolution)
RnP	Rosa nel Pugno (Rose in the Fist)
SA	La Sinistra-l'Arcobaleno (Rainbow Left)
SC	Scelta Civica (Civic Choice)
SD	Sinistra Democratica (Democratic Left)
SDI	Socialisti Democratici Italiani (Italian Democratic Socialists)
SEL	Sinistra, Ecologia, Libertà (The Left, Ecology and Freedom)
SI	Sinistra Italiana (Italian Left)
SME	Società Meridionale di Elettricità
TAV	Treno ad alta velocità (High-speed train)
UD	Unione Democratica (Democratic Union)
UDC	Unione dei Democratici Cristiani e Democratici di Centro (Union of Christian and Centre Democrats)
UdC	Unione di Centro (Union of the Centre)
UDEUR	Unione Democratica per l'Europa (Democratic Union for Europe)
UEFA	Union of European Football Associations
UIL	Italian Labour Union (Unione Italiana del Lavoro)
UK	United Kingdom
USA	United States of America
USSR	Union of Soviet Socialist Republics
VAT	Value-added tax

Timeline

25 July 1943: King Victor Emmanuel III dismisses Benito Mussolini and has him arrested, bringing a formal end to the fascist regime. Marshal Pietro Badoglio appointed as Prime Minister in Mussolini's place with secret orders to negotiate an armistice with the Allies.

8 September 1943: Marshal Badoglio announces that the Cassibile Armistice, signed with the Allies on 3 September, has come into force.

12 September 1943: Germans launch Operation Oak rescuing Mussolini from prison and enabling him to establish a new fascist state in northern Italy, the Italian Social Republic.

27 March 1944: PCI leader, Palmiro Togliatti, returns from exile and promotes the so-called *svolta di Salerno* (known as the Salerno turn after the city that is the seat of Italian government until the Allied liberation of Rome) which will bring his party into government.

24 April 1944: The second Badoglio Government takes office including, for the first time, the parties of the Committee for National Liberation.

4 June 1944: Rome liberated. King Victor Emmanuel transfers his constitutional powers to his son, Umberto, appointing him Lieutenant General of the Realm.

25 June 1944: Decreto Legge Luogotenenziale 151 stipulates that after liberation, the institutions of state are to be decided by a constituent assembly elected by universal suffrage.

28 April 1945: Mussolini summarily executed in the small village of Giulino di Mezzegra having been captured, the previous day, by local partisans while trying to escape to the Swiss border.

16 March 1946: Alcide de Gasperi, now Prime Minister, secures legislation to ensure that the future of the monarchy is to be decided, not by the Constituent Assembly, but by a separate referendum.

9 May 1946: In the hope of influencing public opinion ahead of the referendum, King Victor Emmanuel abdicates in favour of his son Umberto.

2 June 1946: The institutional referendum results in 54% of voters voting in favour of a republic with 46% in favour of retaining the monarchy, while the Constituent Assembly election results in the DC emerging as the largest party with 35% of the vote.

13 June 1946: King Umberto II flies into exile proclaiming those who had sworn loyalty to the King freed from the obligations of their oaths.

28 June 1946: Enrico De Nicola elected as provisional head of state by the Constituent Assembly.

10 February 1947: Treaty of Peace signed between Italy and the victorious powers of the Second World War.

12 March 1947: In an address to a joint session of Congress, US President, Harry S. Truman, fires the starting gun on the Cold War, announcing that "It must be the policy of the United States to support free peoples who are resisting attempted subjugation by armed minorities or by outside pressures".

1 May 1947: Portella della Ginestra massacre sees 11 people killed and 33 wounded during May Day celebrations in Sicily. The presumed killers are the bandit and separatist leader, Salvatore Giuliano and his followers.

12 May 1947: The resignation of De Gasperi as Prime Minister leads to the exclusion from government of the socialists and communists through the formation, without them, of a fourth De Gasperi executive, on 31 May 1947.

1 January 1948: The Constitution of the Italian Republic enters into force.

18 April 1948: At the so-called Christ versus communism election, the Christian Democrats take almost 49% of the vote with 31% for their communist and socialist opponents allied in the Fronte Democratico Popolare (Democratic Popular Front).

11 May 1948: Luigi Einaudi, of the Italian Liberal Party, elected second President of the Italian Republic at the fourth round of voting with 518 votes out of 872.

4 April 1949: Italy joins 11 other countries in signing the North Atlantic Treaty to become one of the founding members of NATO.

10 August 1950: Law no. 646 passed setting up the Cassa per il Mezzogiorno (Fund for the South).

18 April 1951: Italy joins Germany, France and the Benelux countries in signing the Treaty of Paris to give life to the ECSC.

31 March 1953: An electoral law reform, known popularly as the 'Swindle Law' is promulgated provoking considerable public controversy. It provides that the list, or coalition of lists, winning at least 50% of the vote is to be assigned 65% of the seats in the Camera dei Deputati (Chamber of Deputies).

7 June 1953: At the second general election to be held under the new Constitution, the Christian Democrats and their allies fail by less than one percentage point to achieve the required 50% of the vote, while the DC itself suffers a loss of over 8% and the socialists and communists increase their combined support to over 35%.

3 January 1954: Radiotelevisione Italiana makes its first television broadcast.

31 July 1954: The 'Swindle Law' is repealed.

29 April 1955: Christian Democrat, Giovanni Gronchi, elected President of the Republic at the fourth round of voting with 658 votes out of 833.

14 December 1955: United Nations Security Council Resolution 109 recommends Italy for membership of the UN.

4 November 1956: Soviet invasion of Hungary leads to the end of cooperation between the PCI and the PSI with the latter thenceforth looking favourably on the prospect of collaborating with the DC in government.

25 March 1957: Italy signs the Treaty of Rome, becoming a founder member of the EEC.

4 July 1957: The first Fiat 500, symbol of the post-war 'economic miracle', rolls off the production lines.

25 May 1958: The general election sees the DC gain two percentage points with the other parties remaining essentially stable, the only exception being the monarchists whose support declines by some two-thirds.

26 March 1960: A DC minority Government under Fernando Tambroni is sworn in and on 8 April wins the confirmatory vote of confidence in the Chamber of Deputies thanks to the support of the neo-fascist MSI. This provokes widespread public disorder leading to the Government's resignation on 19 July 1960.

6 May 1962: Christian Democrat politician, Antonio Segni, elected President at the ninth round of voting, the votes of the MSI and the monarchists being decisive to the outcome.

11 October 1962: Pope John XXIII opens the Second Vatican Council.

22 October 1962: ENI President, Enrico Mattei, is killed in an air crash during a flight from Sicily to Linate airport, Milan.

5 December 1963: The first Moro Government is sworn in following the general election of 28 April which paves the way for the first DC-led coalition since 1947 to include in the Cabinet representatives of the socialists.

June 26 1964: Rumours begin to circulate concerning Piano Solo, plans for a *coup d'état* drawn up at the instigation of the President of the Republic, apparently as a means of bullying the PSI into sacrificing its more radical demands on the altar of governing cooperation with the DC.

28 December 1964: The Social Democrat, Giuseppe Saragat, is elected President of the Republic at the 21st round of the voting, with 646 votes out of 937, thanks to the decisive support of the communists and the socialists.

24 January 1966: The first occupation of an Italian university takes place when students occupy the Faculty of Sociology at the University of Trento.

19–20 May 1968: The fifth general election to be held under the 1948 Constitution reveals that the reunification of the PSI and the PSDI which had taken place in 1966 is not a paying proposition as the new party takes 14% of the vote, compared to the 20% combined share the two parties had enjoyed in 1963. As a result, the following year the two parties diverge once more.

20 August 1968: Soviet invasion of Czechoslovakia condemned unequivocally by the PCI, underscoring how far it has changed since 1956.

12 December 1969: Bomb explodes at the Banca Nazionale dell'Agricoltura in Piazza Fontana, Milan, killing 17 people and wounding 88.

28 January 1970: The institutions of government of the 'ordinary statute' regions finally become operative—22 years after the regions were provided for by Article 131 of the 1948 Constitution.

20 May 1970: Law no. 300, known as the Workers' Statute, introduces a series of important measures designed to enhance conditions of employment. It is destined to become the cornerstone of the Italian system of labour law.

24 December 1971: Christian Democrat, Giovanni Leone, elected President of the Republic at the 23rd round of voting with 518 votes out of 996.

7–8 May 1972: At the sixth post-war general election, the most noteworthy result is that of the MSI, which doubles its support to take 9% of the vote.

12 May 1974: Referendum on a proposal to abrogate the 1970 Fortuna-Baslini law, providing for divorce, is decisively defeated, with 59.3% of the electorate voting against it.

6 August 1976: Following the 20–21 June general election which sees the PCI make a striking advance to come within four percentage points of the DC, a minority DC Government, under Giulio Andreotti, wins the confirmatory vote of confidence in the Senato della Repubblica (Senate of the Republic) with the abstention of the PCI.

16 March 1978: Aldo Moro kidnapped by the Brigate Rosse (Red Brigades) while on his way to the Chamber of Deputies for a vote of confidence in a new Andreotti Government which, for the first time, would have the support of the PCI.

8 July 1978: Socialist, Sandro Pertini, elected seventh President of the Republic at the 16th round of voting with 832 votes out of 995.

3–4 June 1979: At the eighth post-war general election the PCI retreats by four percentage points to just over 30%, thereby bringing to a definitive end its 'historic compromise' strategy of attempted collaboration with the DC.

2 August 1980: Bombing of Bologna railway station, linked to right-wing extremists, kills 85.

28 June 1981: Giovanni Spadolini of the PRI becomes the first non-DC Prime Minister since December 1945, after the previous DC-led Government is forced to resign owing to the scandal provoked, in March 1981, by the discovery of the Propaganda Due masonic lodge, whose members include a number of high-ranking public servants, politicians and members of the military, and whose activities give it criminal connections.

4 August 1983: Bettino Craxi becomes Italy's first PSI Prime Minister following the 26–27 June general election which sees the DC suffer almost unprecedented losses to take it to a historic low of 33%.

24 June 1985: Christian Democrat, Francesco Cossiga, elected eighth President of the Republic at the first round of voting with 752 votes out of 977.

10 October 1985: Stand-off between US and Italian armed forces at the Sigonella air base in the wake of the Achille Lauro hijacking.

14–15 June 1987: At the general election, the DC recovers slightly to take 34% of the vote, while the PCI continues its downwards slide with 27%.

9 November 1989: Berlin Wall comes down. This leads PCI leader, Achille Ochetto, to announce, on 12 November, that his party will change its name, its symbol and its political programme.

9 June 1991: Referendum proposal to reduce the number of preference votes in Chamber of Deputies elections to one only achieves the support of 95.6% of the vote.

17 February 1992: Mario Chiesa, socialist head of the Milanese old people's home, the Pio Albergo Trivulzio, is caught in the act of accepting a bribe from a cleaning contractor, thus firing the starting gun on the investigations that will lead to the great 'Tangentopoli' ('Bribesville') corruption scandal.

5 April 1992: At the general election (which sees the LN take 8.7% of the vote) the DC's share falls to 29.7%, while the new PDS fails to rise above 16.1%.

25 May 1992: Christian Democrat, Oscar Luigi Scalfaro, elected ninth President of the Republic at the 16th round of voting with 672 votes out of 1,002.

18–19 April 1993: Referendum proposal to abrogate parts of the Senate electoral law (with the aim, thereby, of introducing a majoritarian system) is supported by 82.7% of the voters.

27–28 March 1994: At the general election, the Polo delle Libertà and the Polo del Buon Governo (commonly known as the Polo delle Libertà—Freedom Alliance) win a majority in the Chamber of Deputies and Silvio Berlusconi of FI, its dominant party, becomes Prime Minister for the first time on 11 May.

17 January 1995: Following the collapse of Berlusconi's Government, Lamberto Dini, formerly the Director-General of the Bank of Italy, takes office at the head of republican Italy's first government staffed entirely by non-party technocrats.

21 April 1996: As a result of the general election, L'Ulivo (the Olive Tree), led by Romano Prodi, forms a Government.

22 October 1998: A new Government is formed, under the leadership of Massimo D'Alema of the DS.

1 January 1999: Euro introduced with Italy as one of the first 11 participants in Stage III of Europe's EMU.

13 May 1999: Former Governor of the Bank of Italy, Carlo Azeglio Ciampi, elected 10th President of the Republic at the first round of voting with 707 votes out of 990.

26 April 2000: Following the resignation of the Government in response to a heavy defeat for the governing parties in regional elections, Giuliano Amato, Prime Minister from 1992–93, forms a new administration.

13 May 2001: Berlusconi's Casa delle Libertà (House of Freedoms) coalition sweeps to victory at the general election, winning a clear

majority of seats in both chambers of Parliament. His party, FI, receives almost 30% of the total votes cast.

7 October 2001: For the first time in the history of the Republic, voters are called to the polls to decide whether to confirm changes to the Constitution. The changes in question (concerning the powers of the regions) are supported by 62.4% of the vote on a turnout of just 34%.

10 October 2002: Chamber of Deputies passes the so-called Cirami law (allegedly designed to help the Prime Minister to avoid trial on corruption charges) after a debate which almost sees parliamentarians coming to blows.

17 June 2003: In court on corruption charges, Berlusconi claims that he is the victim of a campaign to discredit him on the part of politically motivated judges and prosecutors.

22 April 2005: Berlusconi receives a presidential mandate to form a new executive. The centre-right's poor performance in the regional elections of 5 April had caused tension within the governing majority forcing Berlusconi to tender his resignation and form a new government with the same allies but with a changed policy focus (especially on taxes).

9–10 April 2006: In legislative elections, the centre-left coalition, L'Unione (the Union), led by the former Prime Minister, Prodi, wins a narrow victory over the Casa delle Libertà in both the Senate and the Chamber of Deputies, and proceeds to form a government composed of nine parties.

10 May 2006: Giorgio Napolitano, a former communist, elected 11th President of the Republic at the fourth round of voting with 543 votes out of 990.

21 February 2007: Prodi submits his resignation as Prime Minister after the Government is defeated in the Senate in a vote on the presence of Italian troops in Afghanistan. On 28 February he regains the premiership after his Government wins votes of confidence in both chambers.

28 October 2007: At a joint conference, the DS and the DL merge to form the PD; the mayor of Rome, Walter Veltroni, is confirmed as the party's National Secretary, having been elected in an open 'primary' election earlier in the month.

20 November 2007: Berlusconi announces the dissolution of FI and the formation of a new centre-right group under his leadership, the PdL. In February 2008 the AN agrees to contest the election under the PdL name, while the LN forms an alliance with the PdL in northern Italy.

17 January 2008: The Minister of Justice, Clemente Mastella, resigns following the arrest of his wife on charges of corruption. Days later he withdraws his party, UDEUR, from the governing coalition, thus depriving it of a majority in the Senate.

24 January 2008: Prodi submits the resignation of his Government, following its defeat in a vote of no confidence in the Senate.

13–14 April 2008: At an early general election, Berlusconi's PdL and its allies win a decisive majority in both chambers, comfortably defeating the PD and IdV.

7 May 2008: A new coalition Government under Berlusconi, comprising the PdL and the LN, is sworn in.

22 July 2008: Legislation granting immunity from prosecution to the holders of Italy's four highest political offices—the President of the Republic, the Prime Minister and the Presidents of both chambers of Parliament—comes into effect. Critics claim that the legislation is designed to protect Berlusconi from prosecution in two separate trials on charges of bribery and of fraud.

29 March 2009: The PdL is formally constituted as a political party, following the dissolution of the AN at a party congress earlier in March.

7 October 2009: The Constitutional Court overturns the legislation of 2008 on immunity from prosecution, on the basis that it violates the principle that all citizens are equal before the law. The court's decision allows both of the criminal cases pending against Berlusconi to be resumed the following month.

30 July 2010: The executive committee of the PdL adopts a motion to censure Gianfranco Fini, the President of the Chamber of Deputies and leader of the AN until its dissolution in 2009, following months of political and personal animosity between him and Berlusconi; Fini's supporters proceed to form a new parliamentary group, FLI, comprising more than 30 deputies, thus weakening the governing majority.

15 November 2010: The four FLI-aligned ministers resign from the Government after Berlusconi rejects a demand by Fini that he resign in order to form a new coalition.

6 April 2011: Berlusconi goes on trial accused of paying for sex with an under-age nightclub dancer, Karima El Mahroug, in 2010.

12–13 June 2011: In a series of referendums called by the parliamentary opposition, four of the Government's legislative measures (on local public services, the revival of nuclear power generation, privatization of water supplies and suspension of legal proceedings for ministers owing to 'legitimate impediment') are overturned by more than

94% of those voting, with the turnout, at 55.5%, being sufficient to render the votes legally binding.

14 September 2011: The Government narrowly wins a vote of confidence in the Chamber of Deputies ensuring the passage of an emergency budget aimed at restoring market confidence in the Italian economy in the context of the sovereign debt crisis in the eurozone. Popular demonstrations take place in protest against the austerity measures, on the grounds that they unfairly target those on lower incomes.

12 November 2011: Following the loss of the Government's majority in the Chamber of Deputies through a number of defections in October and in the face of the escalating economic crisis, Berlusconi—Italy's longest-serving post-war Prime Minister—resigns from office immediately after the approval of another emergency budget.

13 November 2011: President Napolitano appoints Mario Monti, a renowned economist and former EU commissioner, as the country's new Prime Minister; Monti announces the formation of a new Cabinet, composed of a team of 17 technocrats.

26 October 2012: Berlusconi is convicted of tax fraud relating to the purchase of film rights by his company, Mediaset. The former Prime Minister immediately launches an appeal against the verdict, which is upheld in August 2013.

21 December 2012: Following parliamentary approval of the 2013 budget, Monti tenders his resignation as Prime Minister, his Government having lost the parliamentary support of the PdL earlier in December.

24–25 February 2013: There is no clear winner in the general election. The PD and its allies secure a majority of 345 seats in the Chamber of Deputies, but no party or coalition wins a majority in the Senate.

20 April 2013: President Napolitano is elected to an unprecedented second term of office, defeating his opponent, Stefano Rodotà, the candidate proposed by the M5S, by 738 votes to 217.

28 April 2013: A new 'grand coalition' Government is finally sworn in, composed of the PD, the PdL, the UdC and SC. The new administration is headed by Enrico Letta of the PD.

15 November 2013: About 60 PdL members, led by Deputy Prime Minister Angelino Alfano, announce the formation of a new party, the NCD. The following day Berlusconi returns to opposition with a revamped FI. All of the former PdL ministers join the NCD, which remains in the governing coalition.

27 November 2013: The Senate votes to expel Berlusconi following the Court of Cassation's confirmation, on 1 August, of his conviction for tax fraud.

8 December 2013: Matteo Renzi, the Mayor of Florence, is elected to the leadership of the PD from which position, in February 2014, he succeeds in ousting Letta as Prime Minister.

22 February 2014: Renzi takes office as Prime Minister at the head of a coalition chiefly comprising the same parties as had supported the Letta Government.

14 January 2015: President Napolitano announces his resignation, citing his advanced age of 89 years.

3 February 2015: Sergio Mattarella, the candidate of the ruling PD, a judge of the Constitutional Court and former Minister of Defence, is sworn in as President, following four rounds of voting by members of Parliament and regional delegates.

4 May 2015: Proposed electoral reform legislation, known as the Italicum, receives final approval in a parliamentary vote. The reform comes into effect on 1 July 2016.

7 December 2016: Renzi resigns as Prime Minister following the rejection, by 59.1% of voters in a referendum held on 4 December, of proposed constitutional reforms he had promoted.

12 December 2016: President Mattarella asks Paolo Gentiloni of the PD and erstwhile Minister of Foreign Affairs to form a new government. Gentiloni is replaced in the foreign affairs portfolio by Angelino Alfano, and Marco Minniti is appointed Minister of the Interior, although the majority of Cabinet positions remain unchanged.

18 March 2017: Alfano launches a new centre-right party, AP, replacing the NCD which is dissolved.

4 March 2018: At the general election, although no single party secures an overall majority, a surge in anti-establishment and populist sentiment results in the M5S securing 227 and 112 seats in the Chamber of Deputies and the Senate, respectively, and an alliance of the far-right Lega (as LN has been restyled), FdI and FI winning 265 and 137 seats, respectively. A centre-left electoral coalition led by former Prime Minister Matteo Renzi secures just 122 and 60 seats in the two chambers, respectively. Renzi subsequently resigns as leader of the PD and is replaced in an interim capacity by Maurizio Martina.

1 June 2018: After lengthy negotiations, a governing coalition of the Lega and the M5S is sworn in under Giuseppe Conte, a law professor and political novice, as Prime Minister. The leaders of the Lega and the M5S, Matteo Salvini and Luigi Di Maio, assume the posts of Deputy Prime Minister and Minister of the Interior, and Deputy Prime

Minister and Minister of Economic Development and of Labour and Social Policies, respectively.

27 September 2018: The Government announces its budget, which includes a budget deficit target of 2.4% of gross domestic product in 2019 and 2020 (the previous administration had aimed for a 0.8% deficit in 2019), prompting the European Commission to demand revisions owing to Italy's high government debt levels.

26 May 2019: At elections to the European Parliament the Lega wins 28 seats, the PD 19, the M5S 14 and FI six.

20 August 2019: Prime Minister Conte tenders his resignation, accusing Lega leader and Deputy Prime Minister Salvini of creating a political crisis by withdrawing his support for the governing coalition in order to precipitate a general election for opportunistic purposes following the League's dramatic advance at the May European Parliament elections.

5 September 2019: Following negotiations, a new coalition, chiefly comprising the M5S, the PD and LeU, is sworn in under Conte.

17 September 2019: Former Prime Minister Renzi announces that he is leaving the PD in order to form a new party, Italia Viva which, although it remains part of the governing coalition has the support of a sufficiently large number of parliamentarians potentially to deprive the Government of its majority.

26 January 2020: Regional elections in Emilia Romagna and Calabria see the centre-left retain their traditional stronghold, while support for the M5S collapses in both regions.

9 March 2020: In view of the growing threat from the pandemic of coronavirus disease (COVID-19), the Government extends lockdown measures to the whole of Italy.

1 Introduction

Italian politics in early 2020

In early 2020 Italy was ruled by a coalition, which, unusually for an Italian government, appeared to be rather strong. Voting intention polls suggested that support for the governing parties had been stable for several weeks, while other surveys suggested that Prime Minister Giuseppe Conte's personal approvals ratings had increased markedly.[1] The opposition parties were under pressure to ensure that their criticisms were constructive. This was hardly surprising. The pandemic of coronavirus disease (COVID-19) was killing approximately 600 people per day; the health service in parts of the country was struggling to cope; schools, offices and factories were closed; and citizens were confined to their homes. The tendency for incumbent governments to enjoy unusually high levels of popular support at times of national emergency is well known.

In early 2020, therefore, the Italian Government's hold on office seemed much more secure than it had done at the beginning of the year. Then, governing together had meant that the parties of the ruling coalition were involved in a prisoner's dilemma. That is, the action each had to take to advance its own interests could not but damage their joint interest in remaining stably in office.

First, there was the MoVimento 5 Stelle (M5S—Five Star Movement), an anti-establishment protest party, founded in 2009, which initially came to prominence in local elections in 2012. Since it sought the support of voters from across the political spectrum, it had always refused to locate itself in left-right terms and so lacked a clear ideological profile. Consequently, it was struggling to retain support. In government since its triumph at the general election of 2018, it gave the appearance of being absorbed by the very political system it had promised protesters it would overhaul. Regional elections had suggested that its right-wing voters were deserting it for the populist chauvinism of the opposition Lega (League), while its left-wing voters were refusing to turn out. Under pressure, therefore, to take political initiatives that would stem the outflow of support, its leader, the Minister of Foreign Affairs Luigi Di Maio, could not help taking stances that often provoked tensions with his governing partners.

Second, there was Italia Viva, a party formed the previous September to further the political ambitions of its founder, the former Prime Minister, Matteo Renzi. Offering up as the basis for his party's appeal a modernization narrative built around the ideas of equal opportunities; embracing the challenges of globalization; cosmopolitanism, and further European integration, he had a sufficient number of parliamentary seats to deprive the Government of a majority. However, he had not been able to garner support for his party in the country above single figures. To avoid political marginalization he had sought, like the M5S, political visibility at every turn, supporting the Government, yes, but being critical and goading his partners at every opportunity.

Finally, there was the Partito Democratico (PD—Democratic Party), a centre-left party under Lazio regional president, Nicola Zingaretti, formed in 2007 through an amalgamation of ex-communists and former Christian democrats. As such, it too suffered from the lack of a clear ideological profile around which it might construct a solid base of support. However, it could do little to try to develop one, as it had to spend most of its time in government firefighting by mediating between a modernizing Renzi and an anti-establishment Di Maio, both of whom were in search of visibility.

In opposition were the three parties, which, in 2018, had tried but narrowly failed to win an overall majority as an electoral coalition of the centre-right. The largest was the League, which had emerged at the beginning of the 1990s as a regional autonomy party called the Lega Nord (Northern League). Since Matteo Salvini had become its leader in December 2013 at the age of 40, it had sought to reinvent itself as a right-wing nationalist party, dropping the word 'northern' from its name in 2018 in order to extend its appeal to the country as a whole. The second largest party, under the 43-year-old Georgia Meloni, was Fratelli d'Italia (Brothers of Italy), whose ideological and organizational roots could be traced back to the neo-fascist Movimento Sociale Italiano (Italian Social Movement) formed in 1946. Finally, there was Silvio Berlusconi's Forza Italia (Forward Italy, or Come on Italy!), formed in 1994 as a means of defending the entrepreneur's economic interests by bringing together, in that year's elections, a coalition of parties capable of defeating the left. Once Italy's largest party, it had gone into decline since its founder had lost the premiership in 2011 and by late 2019 it was polling in single figures.

In short, Italian party politics in early 2020 seemed rather straight-forward (Table 1.1). On the one hand, a governing coalition, securely in office, commanded 348 of the 630 seats in the Camera dei Deputati (Chamber of Deputies) and 164 of the 321 seats in the Senato della Repubblica (Senate of the Republic). Opposing it was a cohesive coalition of the centre-right led by Salvini's League.

Appearances were deceptive, however. For one thing, the party system was far from being stable. Aggregate electoral volatility had been on an upward trend since the beginning of the 1980s and in 2013 and 2018 it had been higher than at any other election since the Second World War with the sole exception of 1994 (Emanuele and Chiaramonte, 2020, fig. 2). From that year, elections had been bipolar competitions between party coalitions, of the centre-left and centre-right, each competing for overall majorities of seats. This had ended in 2013 with the explosive growth of a significant third force, the above-mentioned M5S, thus considerably complicating the process of government formation.

Underlying the instability was the chronic weakness of the political parties, that is, their lack of stable and extensive extra-parliamentary organizations and their lack of public authority. Because of this, and because they were having to appeal to an increasingly volatile electorate, they had come to operate with increasingly short-term horizons and were

Table 1.1 Governing and opposition parties in the Chamber of Deputies and Senate, number of seats, early 2020

	Chamber of Deputies	Senate
Governing parties		
Five Star Movement	203	98
Democratic Party	88	35
Liberi e Uguali	11	5
Italia Viva	30	17
Others	12	15
Opposition parties		
League	125	60
Fratelli d'Italia	35	18
Forza Italia	97	61
Others	19	9
Total seats	630	321

Source: author's compilation based on data provided by the Chamber of Deputies (www.camera.it/leg18/46) and the Senate (www.senato.it/leg/18/BGT/Schede/Gruppi/Grp.html).

consequently unable to develop agreed-upon long-term strategies for the future of the country. A good example of this was the debate that had surrounded the so-called plastic tax as part of the previous autumn's budget discussions. A reasonable observer might have expected the debate to focus on the role of the tax in a strategy for tackling the climate change that has since been implicated in the spread of COVID-19.[2] Instead, it focused almost exclusively on the immediate-term costs of the tax for consumers, on the potential political costs for the parties, and therefore on what additional measures could be taken to offset them.

The country's political weaknesses, then, constituted significant obstacles in the way of the development of strategies for overcoming its economic and social problems, of which two stood out. The first was the lack of growth. Since 1990 growth rates have been much below what they were 45 years after the end of the war and below those of the other large European countries and the USA. This is a problem because the period from 1970 saw a number of important economic and social changes, described later in the book, which initiated a long-term upward trend in the level of public debt. By 2014 it had reached 135% of gross domestic product (GDP), and it has remained at around this level ever since. Consequently, Italian governments find themselves in a catch-22 situation. High levels of debt and the large proportions of tax revenue that must be spent on interest payments considerably limit the scope for using public expenditure to stimulate growth. A lack of growth makes it difficult to pay down the public debt.

Inward investment, as an alternative source of growth, is difficult to attract owing to inefficiencies in the legal and administrative systems. Vested interests often stand in the way of reform. For example, in 2006 the Minister for Economic Development, Pierluigi Bersani, sought to remove restrictions on competition in a number of markets including that for taxi services. However, in the latter case a ferocious drivers' strike that had the tacit support of the then leader of the opposition, Berlusconi, forced the minister partially to retreat. There are huge political obstacles in the way of attempts to reduce the debt through tax rises and spending cuts. They include unemployment (at 9.7% in September 2019), absolute poverty (affecting over 5m. people in that year) and a level of GDP per capita which in 2018 was still below the level it had reached just before the global financial crash in 2008. The annual budget round provides an opportunity for opposition parties, during parliamentary discussions, to exploit divisions between spending ministers, thus exerting additional spending pressure.

Second, the country has an ageing population. This has put pressure on the pensions system. On 7 March 2018 the European Commission published its annual country report on Italy, noting that the old-age dependency ratio stood at 34.3% and was forecast to exceed 60% by 2045 as the country's fertility rate was set to remain low. Meanwhile, thanks to the 'brain drain', net immigration had been declining and in the poorer southern regions it was negative (European Commission, 2018). Many argue, therefore, that immigration is essential to helping Italy to overcome its economic problems, especially to ensure the sustainability of the pensions system, since immigrants are on average younger than Italians and have a higher fertility rate.

Once again, politics gets in the way. Since 2008 austerity and refugee crises have made it possible for the League to make political capital by drawing on popular resentments to convince large numbers of citizens that migration represents a security threat. Measures to stem migrant flows have done little to stop the spread of intolerance and xenophobia. In February 2017 PD Minister of the Interior, Marco Minniti, signed an agreement with Libya providing for the financing and training of the Libyan coastguard. Sea arrivals and asylum applications, which in 2017 had numbered 119,369 and 130,119, respectively, fell to 23,370 and 53,596, respectively, in 2018 (Geddes and Pettrachin, 2020, fig. 4). Nevertheless, in the same year, after a general election campaign dominated by the issue of immigration, support for the League reached an all-time high and support for the PD an all-time low.

Therefore, in early 2020 Italy was a country whose political parties stood as significant obstacles in the way of resolution of its social and economic problems, and the purpose of this book is to help the reader to understand how Italian politics has reached this point. It does this by tracing the most significant processes of political, economic and social change to have marked Italian history in recent years back to their roots in the Italian political system as it emerged at the end of the Second World War. The book therefore provides a narrative. Narratives provide understanding, because they are stories that tell us who we are, where we have come from, where we are now, and where we are going. In *As You Like It*, William Shakespeare wrote:

> All the world's a stage,
> And all the men and women merely players;
> They have their exits and their entrances;
> And one man in his time plays many parts,
> His acts being seven ages.

What makes these lines so moving and profound is that they draw our attention to the fact that we cannot relate to the world around us *but* through narratives (as a result of which we experience our lives—and therefore history itself—as a process of forward movement through a series of stages). In their broadest sense, then, narratives are ubiquitous. All organizations have them. Without them, we would find it impossible to make sense of the world or of our place in it. Whether we are aware of it or not, it is by virtue of the various narratives that we have come to believe in that we are able to engage with others as competent social actors.

Narratives of the kind developed in this book are of more than just academic relevance, as the following episode reveals. In early 2020 one of the most significant issues dominating public discussion in Italy was the European Union's (EU) response to the COVID-19 outbreak. It was clear that the Italian economy would contract sharply and that the level of public debt would spiral massively. Consequently, on 17 March Giuseppe Conte had called for the issue of European recovery bonds, and in early April, he had suggested that the EU risked collapsing unless it rose to the challenge of coming up with a coordinated economic and social response to the COVID-19 outbreak. His words did not seem hyperbolic. On the one hand, his interlocutors representing Germany, Austria, Finland and the Netherlands seemed to think that support for the mutualization of debt involved in the bonds might damage their standing with their domestic electorates to the advantage of growing 'sovereigntist' and populist forces. On the other hand, they were almost certainly aware that failure to support them risked fuelling 'sovereigntist' forces in Italy and her allies. Either way, therefore, the European integration project itself appeared to be at risk (as it had done eight years earlier when the sovereign debt crisis provoked resistance to austerity in debtor countries and popular resentment against financial aid packages in the creditor countries).

In seeking to reach a compromise that would avoid such an outcome, negotiators were probably aware that they were playing a 'two-level game' (Putnam, 1988). That is, if their domestic political circumstances affected the positions they could take in the Eurogroup and the European Council, then the outcome of negotiations there would affect their standing at home. They would therefore have to consider both how any stance they took might play with their domestic audiences, and the implications of such a stance for the domestic audiences of the other side as this would affect that side's ability to get any deals ratified.

It is for this reason that knowledge of the history and the workings of other countries' politics are so essential to diplomats. When their interlocutors say to them, "I'd like to sign, but I would never be able to get Parliament to agree to it" (or words to that effect), they need to know if such claims are credible. The above-mentioned episode revealed, in short, that Italy's domestic politics had relevance for audiences far beyond the country's borders, well outside the walls of academia. It is for this reason, among others, that I think that the tale I have to tell in this book is an important one.

Notes

1 Agenzia Italia, 'L'emergenza coronavirus fa crescere (ancora) la popolarità di Conte', 27 March 2020, www.agi.it/blog-italia/youtrend/post/2020-03-27/supermedia-sondaggi-supermedia-conte-lega-pd-7903939/.
2 See, for example, the European Public Health Alliance website, available at https://epha.org/coronavirus-threat-greater-for-polluted-cities/. It appears that the health threat of COVID-19 is on average greater for those exposed to higher levels of air pollution. This may be because living in polluted areas reduces patients' capacity to fight off infections and because dust particles act as vehicles for the transmission of the virus from person to person over extended distances.

2 A 'blocked' political system
Politics in the 'First Republic'

Benito Mussolini's dismissal and arrest on 25 July 1943 took place quickly and without violence. The reason for this was that by that date the country's elites were looking for a way to extract Italy from the war, and they had the population on their side. By then, the Allies had landed in Sicily; their aerial bombardments were becoming increasingly frequent; and there was all-round economic hardship. Strikes in a number of factories in northern Italy brought it home to King Victor Emmanuel III that popular support for the regime was ebbing fast and that he would have to cut his ties with the fascists if he wanted to avoid being faced by 'an insurrectionary movement founded on the fraternization of troops and civilians' (Ginsborg, 1990: 12). What took place, therefore, was in effect a military coup that prevented any kind of fascist resistance to Mussolini's defenestration. For ordinary Italians, however, the event brought a sense of real confusion. It represented the demise of the man who had given them their sense of nationhood. It led to German troops pouring into Italy from the north and to the emergence of the Resistance movement organized by the anti-fascist parties in the Comitato di Liberazione Nazionale (CLN—Committee for National Liberation). It led to Mussolini's replacement by a government that became a puppet of the Allies who were advancing from the south. On 3 September the Government had signed a secret armistice with the Allies, which, when it became public on 8 September, led to the disintegration of the army that had been left with no orders other than to cease hostilities with the Allies and to resist attacks from all other quarters. The Germans, in reaction, had taken over Rome, snatched Mussolini from prison and set him up as the puppet dictator of the Repubblica di Salò (Republic of Salò) in the north. The King, meanwhile, had fled Rome and reinstalled his government in Allied-controlled southern Italy. In this context, there was confusion as to the locus of power and authority, uncertainty as to what would happen next and a complete lack of clarity about where, precisely, the loyalties of the patriotic Italians were now supposed to lie.

Under these circumstances, the Roman Catholic Church on the one hand and the anti-fascist parties on the other quickly became rallying points for working out ideas and attitudes. The church had deep roots in civil society through its parishes and collateral associations. However, popular backing for the Resistance gave legitimacy and authority to the anti-fascist parties dominating it. The largest of these were the Partito Comunista Italiano (PCI—Italian Communist Party)—whose origins went back to the Bolshevik Revolution and a split in the Partito Socialista Italiano (PSI—Italian Socialist Party) in 1921—and the Democrazia Cristiana (DC—Christian Democrats) that was formed in 1942 as a revival of the earlier Partito Popolare Italiano (Italian People's Party). The growth of political participation arising from the Resistance turned the parties into mass-based organizations, and this enabled them to penetrate the interstices of civil society and the state, enabling them to become the main channels for the transmission of resources from centre to periphery.

On the one hand, the parties acquired significant influence over the reconstruction of social organizations and interest groups, enabling those such as the DC and the PCI to use the groups as party flanking organizations and so to establish territorially based political subcultures. The Catholic subculture in the north-eastern regions of Friuli-Venezia Giulia, Veneto, and Trentino-Alto Adige/Südtirol (where under the Austrian empire prior to unification the local clergy had defended Italian nationalism) enabled the DC to establish a stronghold there. The Marxist subculture in the central regions of Emilia-Romagna, Tuscany, Umbria and Marche (where oppressive rule under the Papal States meant that the movement for unification had been driven by anti-clerical sentiments, thus favouring the subsequent rise of socialism) underpinned the hegemony there of the PCI. On the other hand, if interest group ties and the subcultures shored up popular support for the parties, then the latter became a favoured channel through which some of the most influential groups sought to communicate with decision-makers. Consequently, instead of aggregating demands, the parties often acted as instruments of the groups, transmitting to government sectional demands—and thus helping to sustain a tendency for power to be managed in clientelistic ways.

A good example of this phenomenon was the relationship enjoyed by the small farmers' organization, Coldiretti, with the DC. Created by the party's Paolo Bonomi in October 1944, Coldiretti had representatives who were members of the party's governing bodies and were regularly elected, as DC candidates, to the Parlamento (Parliament). Here they could pursue legislation of interest to the organization by taking advantage, among other things, of the power that Article 72 of the Constitution gives to each chamber of Parliament to confer law-making powers upon its committees, where micro-sectional legislation could be pursued relatively free from the public gaze. On the other hand, Coldiretti's control of the agricultural consortia, relevant for a range of farmers' economic activities, meant that it had great vote-mobilizing prowess. Farmers could not afford not to be a member of the organization and voted the way they were told to because of the preference vote. The American political scientist, Joseph LaPalombara, explained it thus:

> Peasant farmers in each district are told what combination of preference-vote numbers to cast. While this method does not completely destroy secrecy of the ballot, it does give the leadership an opportunity to gauge how closely each district adheres to the line established by the leaders. Where deviation is too pronounced, retaliatory measures can be taken.
>
> (1964: 242)

Clientelism had roots which went back to the failure of the 1861 unification to produce an effective nationally integrating ideology, and therefore to the difficulties of the state in asserting its authority against unofficial power centres and local elites (and, in extreme cases, organizations like the Mafia), which sought to manipulate public institutions to their own advantage. Unification of the peninsula had, after all, essentially been an elite-driven process, the product of an alliance between the southern gentry and a northern bourgeoisie, both in search of order. It had been opposed by the church. In the context of widespread illiteracy and an extremely limited franchise, ideals of national unity were unable to engage the enthusiasm of more than very small minorities, and the population's allegiances remained strictly parochial. In the post-Second World War period, southern poverty—by sustaining mistrust and thus undermining the potential for collective action—also played a role, as did the dependence of southern economic activity on the state for its implantation and development. By enhancing their rivalry, the new institutions of representative democracy ensured that politicians would retain power only to the degree that they successfully supplied the clientelistic favours that their voters sought. Against this background, the specific features of the post-war party system made a decisive contribution to the maintenance of clientelism, as we shall see.

Mussolini's dismissal in 1943 had led the King to appoint as Prime Minister Marshal Pietro Badoglio who, following the armistice and under pressure from the Soviet Union and the Allies, broadened the base of his government, in April 1944, to include the CLN parties. This would prevent the Resistance from being able to claim that it was the legitimate political authority in the liberated regions of the north. This served the interests of both the Allies and the Soviets, whose aims of dividing Europe into spheres of influence required, in the Italian case, maintenance of the *status quo ante*. Consequently, the process of transition from the fascist to the post-war regime was one of continuity as well as of change.

The elements of continuity were four in number. First, the process of political change never escaped the control of the traditional elites. Badoglio was replaced in June 1944 by a series of civilian Prime Ministers—Ivanoe Bonomi, Ferruccio Parri and then the Christian Democrats' Alcide de Gasperi whose government presided over the Constituent Assembly elections and the referendum on the monarchy of 2 June 1946. Efforts by the Parri Government (21 June–8 December 1945) to purge the state administration of its fascist elements were hampered by the Government's dependence on its administrators for the acquittal of its business and by popular protest at the perceived injustice of the way it was being carried out. The subsequent De Gasperi Government (10 December 1945–1 July 1946) 'replaced virtually all of the Prefects and police chiefs which had been appointed in the North by the CLN. In this way it completed the process of securing the continuity of the state machine and its triumph over the Resistance' (Newell, 2010a: 24). Finally, in the state of confusion that followed the fall of *il Duce*, even while many concluded that the Resistance offered redemption and the only *patria* worth having, others (having made a heavy psychological investment in Mussolini and his promises) were unable to conclude that the dictatorship had been a foolish mistake. Still others identified with the King. Consequently, for several decades after the war, neo-fascist and monarchist parties representing the so-called *nostalgici* (the nostalgic) regularly shared about 7% of the vote on average. Their status as pariah parties was confirmed by the one occasion on which a government attempted to hold office by relying on their votes in Parliament. This was the case of the minority DC government, under Fernando Tambroni, which held office from 25 March to 26 July 1960 and was forced to resign in the wake of street demonstrations that were ferociously repressed by the police. The episode was a symbol of the persistence of pockets of authoritarianism that out-lived the fall of fascism. Another of these was the continued enforcement of the fascist penal code, which, although incompatible with the fundamental rights and liberties set out in Part 1 of the new Constitution could not initially be struck down for want of a constitutional court, as we shall see.

However, none of this could diminish the significance of the elements of rupture and change: the abolition of the monarchy; the establishment of democracy; the drafting of the Constitution; and the establishment of anti-fascism as the founding ideology of the post-war political system. These were real and important achievements. The elimination of royal power, by 12,717,923 votes (54.2 %) to 10,719,284 (45.8 %), brought the end of a dynasty which besides having been complicit in the rise of fascism had always shown scant regard for democracy. In many respects, the achievements exceeded the standards found elsewhere. The Constitution, for example, reflected liberal principles and asserted, besides the usual civil and political rights characteristic of a democracy, a series of social rights—to work (Article 4), to health care (Article 32), to education (Article 34), to training (Article 35) etc.—that continue to compare favourably with those found in the constitutions of other liberal democracies.

That this is the case is due to the composition and the goals of the members of the Constituent Assembly, whose election had been secured by the CLN parties in June 1944. Then, as the price of their participation in government, they had succeeded in obliging the monarchy to agree to a sort of provisional constitution, the Decreto Legge Luogoteneziale 25 Giugno 1944 no. 151. This stipulated that after liberation, the institutions of state would be decided by a Constituent Assembly elected by universal suffrage to decide upon a new Constitution, and that in the meantime the legislative function would be exercised by the Government. Thanks to the latter provision, in March 1946 De Gasperi, now Prime Minister, was able to secure legislation providing that the future of the monarchy would be decided not by the Assembly but by a separate referendum. Thus, his party would be spared the considerable damage that would have been inflicted upon it due to the fact that while its spokespersons were for the most part republicans, its voters were, by and large, monarchists (Ginsborg, 1990: 91). This was a division that could not have been hidden in an assembly but could be so hidden in the context of a referendum where the party could, and did, remain officially neutral. The legislation also stipulated that in the event of a victory for the republic, a new head of state would be chosen by the Constituent Assembly, as happened on 28

June 1946 with the election of the liberal jurist, Enrico De Nicola, as provisional head of state (and first President of the Italian Republic from 1 January 1948). The event was significant in that it again symbolized the 'continuity of the state', and from that perspective it was conservative in its implications, representing, as it did, the process of seamless transition from the fascist to the republican regimes.

The goals of the constituents reflected the political context in which the Assembly was elected and obliged to deliberate. It was essentially dominated by the DC on the one hand and the PCI and the PSI on the other (Table 2.1). After it had begun its work, US President, Harry Truman, fired the starting gun on the Cold War with an address to the US Congress on 12 March 1947. In it, he announced a shift in US foreign policy away from viewing the Soviet Union as an anti-fascist ally towards preventing communist expansion wherever it might occur. Foreign and domestic policy are never completely separate sectors; however, in the Italian case, at this historical juncture, international affairs were decisive for domestic politics since the one basic question underlying all party disputes was the parties' attitudes towards the USA on the one hand and the USSR on the other (Chabod, 1961: 160– 61). Consequently, in May 1947 the PCI and the PSI were expelled from the Italian Government, thus bringing to an end the collaboration between the anti-fascist parties that had been initiated in the CLN in July 1943. As a result, the deliberations of the Constituent Assembly became driven by the concerns of those on either side of the Cold War

Table 2.1 Constituent Assembly elections 2 June 1946

Party lists	Votes (no.)	Votes (%)	Seats
Christian Democrats	8,101,004	32.21	207
Italian Socialist Party of Proletarian Unity	4,758,129	20.68	115
Italian Communist Party	4,356,686	18.93	104
National Democratic Union	1,560,638	6.78	41
Everyman's Front	1,211,956	5.27	30
Italian Republican Party	1,003,007	4.36	23
National Bloc for Freedom	637,328	2.77	16
Others	1,381,731	9.00	20
Total	23,010,479	100.00	556

Source: author's compilation based on data available from the Ministry of the Interior at https://elezionistorico.interno.gov.it/.

left/right divide, to guarantee themselves against the potential author-itarianism of those on the other (Hine, 1981: 64). Thus, besides divid-ing power between the legislative, executive and judicial branches of the state and establishing sub-national tiers of government, the Constitution places a number of restrictions, unusual from a com-parative perspective, on central executive power. First, the two bran-ches of the legislature, the Camera dei Deputati (Chamber of Deputies) and the Senato della Repubblica (Senate of the Republic), have iden-tical legislative powers and in order to remain in office governments must retain the confidence of both. Second, governments cannot decide, on their own authority, the priority their bills will be given in the parliamentary timetable, which is instead drawn up by each cham-ber's committee of parliamentary party group leaders. Third, bills, once introduced, must be considered in committee, where they may be amended, before being voted on by the House. Consequently, from a comparative perspective, the success rate of government bills is low (Newell, 2006). Having agreed the Constitution, which came into force on 1 January 1948, its drafters then found themselves at loggerheads in the general election held on 18 April 1948. Subsequently famous as the 'Christ versus communism' election, it saw Pope Pius XII declaring that anyone who failed to vote to deny victory to the Popular Democratic Front, the electoral alliance of the PCI and the PSI, would be com-mitting 'a grave sin, a mortal transgression', while the Americans threatened to deny Italy Marshall Aid in the event of a victory of the left.

Not surprisingly, then, the Cold War divide by which the Constitu-tion's drafters were separated, for long prevented its effective imple-mentation in many instances. Thus, regional administrations, provided for by Article 114 were not fully legislated for until the late 1960s and the early 1970s. The DC was fearful that the regions might provide a power base for the PCI bearing in mind that while the latter was a 'pariah' at national level, other parties were often willing to work with it in government at the local level. Second, having convincingly defeated the left in 1948 and again at the election in 1953, the con-servative forces in Parliament ensured that the enabling legislation set-ting up the Constitutional Court contained a provision 'that the five judges chosen by parliament (out of a total of fifteen) should be elected by a three-fifths majority'. This enabled the Government 'either to pack the court with conservative judges or, if it failed to win a major-ity, to prevent the court from starting its work by ensuring that no candidates obtained the necessary three-fifths majority in parliament'. Following the outcome of the 1953 election, 'the parties adopted the latter course, and the deliberate obstructionism which followed ensured that the court was ready to hand down its first judgement only in 1956' (Hine, 1981: 66).

The development of the Cold War led—following the 1956 Soviet invasion of Hungary and the division between the PCI and the PSI that resulted—to the *conventio ad excludendum*, the refusal of the DC or any of the other parties from the PSI rightwards to be involved in any kind of alliance with the communists. Thus, excluded from any possibility of joining the Government, the PCI was joined in permanent opposition by the neo-fascist Movimento Sociale Italiano (Italian Social Movemvement) that was formed in 1946 by former junior officials of the Repubblica di Salò—also regarded as a pariah party. Under these circumstances, the DC emerged at every election until 1994 as the largest party, able to capitalize on voters' fears of the left and right extremes—able, that is, to attract votes from both sides of the political spectrum as the main bulwark against both the communists and the fascists. It was, therefore, the mainstay of all feasible governing coalitions. Moreover, as exclusion of left and right rendered impossible bipolar party competition and Westminster-style alternation in office, governing coalitions were decided only after election results had been declared, and therefore parties' relative parliamentary strengths were known. That is, with voting taking place according to the open-list system of proportional representation in large multi-member constituencies, governing formulae were as much the product of the *ex post* decisions of the parties in Parliament as of the *ex ante* decisions of voters. The consequence was that the DC found itself permanently in office governing in coalition with shifting combinations of the parties—the Partito Socialista Democratico Italiano (PSDI—Italian Social Democratic Party), the Partito Repubblicano Italiano (PRI—Italian Republican Party), the Partito Liberale Italiano (PLI—Italian Liberal Party) and (from 1963) the Partito Socialista Italiano (PSI—Italian Socialist Party)—to its immediate left and right.

Of these parties, the Social Democrats had come into being in January 1947 when socialists wanting a non-Stalinist, reformist party able to operate autonomously of the communists had split from the PSI—encouraged to do so both by the DC (which thereby gained a moderate coalition partner) and by the PCI (which gained an ally that had rid itself of any anti-communist elements). The Social Democrats themselves were condemned to remain a small minority. As they were unable to exercise any influence other than as a potential coalition partner of the DC, they rapidly degenerated into a party with few distinctive ideals and fully immersed in the politics of clientelism. Both the PRI and the PLI remained small thanks to the ability of the DC to dominate the centre-right of the political spectrum which these parties also occupied. That left the PSI, which in broad terms followed in the footsteps of the Social Democrats in that having broken with the PCI in the aftermath of 1956, it too was inevitably sucked into the orbit of the DC, a process culminating in its formal entry into government in December 1963. If the socialists themselves saw government participation as an opportunity to effect what they referred to as 'structural reforms', then for most in the DC, by separating the PSI from the PCI, it offered the opportunity to further the process of the left's isolation that had begun with the earlier emergence of the PSDI. Participation in government cost the PSI a further split (this time to its left). It also led—through an apparent conspiracy that came to be known as the Piano Solo—to veiled threats (involving President Antonio Segni and the head of the Carabinieri, General Giovanni De Lorenzo) that anything less than its compliance in supporting a government that turned out to be driven by anything but reforming zeal, might provoke a crisis of Italian democracy itself. Following this first bruising experience of government, the PSI found itself trapped by the same dilemma that the Social Democrats had found themselves in. Consequently, the party spent the next 30 years very firmly confined to a 9%–15% share of the vote and in constant search of a profile to enable it to distinguish itself from its larger competitors to its right and left as its idealism too gradually faded.

The power of the Christian Democrats, meanwhile, was to a very significant extent, self-reinforcing. Thus, as a centre party, it had an especially elastic ideology that enabled it to appeal to a broad spectrum of voters. Its widespread appeal enabled it to give substance to its claim to be the most effective bulwark against communism, which in turn enabled it to count on the conspicuous ideological and economic resources of two enormously significant actors: the Roman Catholic Church and the US government. If these resources helped it to remain large, then this in turn enabled it to control public resources that would allow it to maintain a large following through which it could retain a degree of autonomy from powerful actors such as the church or the employers' organization, Confindustria. Hence, although it was a Catholic party it was never a confessional party. While it supported capitalism, it was not a champion of unregulated free markets. Nor was it a monolithic entity. On the contrary, as a large party that had successfully penetrated large areas of the state and society for the purposes of resource distribution, it became an arena for competing factions, each with a power of veto when some external event necessitated some policy initiative on the part of the Government.

The impossibility of bipolar alternation reduced the pressure that there might otherwise have been on governing coalitions to pursue coherent legislative programmes, and thus their capacity to maintain the cohesion, and the discipline of parliamentary followers, that would have been required to make coherent policymaking possible in the first place. The upshot was considerable government instability (there were 46 changes of government between 1948 and 1994; see Table 2.2) as parties unable to develop distinct policy profiles or take decisive initiatives were reduced instead to arguing over the distribution of offices to be used to maintain electoral followings by being exploited for clientelistic purposes. This situation had three major consequences for the political system as a whole.

First, the politics of clientelism meant that entrepreneurs were dependent on the favour of politicians for a range of routine business matters—from town planning decisions to those concerning the awarding of public works contracts—while being deprived of the leg-islative certainty needed for sound investment decisions. They conse-quently sought to establish stable relationships with politicians whereby, in exchange for financial support at a time when the cost of politics was rising, they would obtain more of the certainty needed for finance and investment to be managed and planned rationally. There therefore developed a whole series of improper relations between eco-nomic and political power—including concomitants like the infamous Propaganda Due masonic lodge, exposed in 1981, implicated in numerous crimes, and sometimes described as 'a state within a state'—giving rise to veritable clans whose purpose was nothing other than mutual assistance in the management and enhancement of the power of their members.

Second, clientelism went hand in hand with *partitocrazia*—the gov-erning parties' control of nominations to public positions spanning the hierarchy from ministers to the humblest of local government offi-cials—and this eventually weakened the parties organizationally. It provided fertile ground for factional competition for the control of resources, and undermined the quality of the grassroots membership—shifting the predominant motives for joining from the ideological to the venal so that the parties began to lack members who were pos-sessed of the commitment necessary for maintaining effectiveness among the population at large.

Third, by turning rights into favours, the politics of clientelism sus-tained popular cynicism and resentment, which eventually made itself felt in the polling booths. As constellations of specific interests rather than united organizations with general goals, the governing parties'

Table 2.2 Governments of the first republican period, 1948–94

Government	Dates	Composition	Duration (in days)
1st legislature, 8 May 1948–4 April 1953 (general election: 18 April 1948)			
De Gasperi V	23 May 1948–12 Jan. 1950	DC, PLI, PSLI, PRI	599
De Gasperi VI	27 Jan. 1950–16 July 1951	DC, PSLI, PRI	535
De Gasperi VII	26 July 1951–29 June 1953	DC, PRI	704
2nd legislature, 25 June 1953–14 March 1958 (general election: 7 June 1953)			
De Gasperi VIII	16 July 1953–28 July 1953	DC	12
Pella	17 August 1953–5 Jan. 1954	DC	141
Fanfani I	18 Jan. 1954–30 Jan. 1954	DC	12
Scelba	10 Feb. 1954–22 June 1955	DC, PSDI, PLI	497
Segni I	6 July 1955–6 May 1957	DC, PSDI, PLI	670
Zoli	19 May 1957–19 June 1958	DC	396
3rd legislature, 12 June 1958–18 February 1963 (general election: 25 May 1958)			
Fanfani II	1 July 1958–26 Jan. 1959	DC, PSDI	209
Segni II	15 Feb. 1959–24 Feb. 1960	DC	374
Tambroni	25 March 1960–19 July 1960	DC	116
Fanfani III	26 July 1960–2 Feb. 1962	DC	556
Fanfani IV	21 Feb. 1962–16 May 1963	DC, PSDI, PRI	449
4th legislature, 16 May 1963–11 March 1968 (general election: 28 April 1963)			
Leone I	21 June 1963–5 Nov. 1963	DC	137
Moro I	4 Dec. 1963–26 June 1964	DC, PSI, PSDI, PRI	205
Moro II	22 July 1964–21 Jan. 1966	DC, PSI, PSDI, PRI	548
Moro III	23 Feb. 1966–5 June 1968	DC, PSI, PSDI, PRI	833
5th legislature, 5 June 1968–28 February 1972 (general election: 19 May 1968)			
Leone II	24 June 1968–19 Nov. 1968	DC	148
Rumor I	12 Dec. 1968–5 July 1969	DC, PSU, PRI	205
Rumor II	5 August 1969–7 Feb. 1970	DC	186
Rumor III	27 March 1970–6 July 1970	DC, PSI, PSDI, PRI	101
Colombo	6 August 1970–15 Jan. 1972	DC, PSI, PSDI, PRI	527
Andreotti I	17 Feb. 1972–26 Feb. 1972	DC	9
6th legislature, 25 May 1972–1 May 1976 (general election: 7–8 May 1972)			
Andreotti II	26 June 1972–12 June 1973	DC, PSDI, PLI	351
Rumor IV	7 July 1973–2 March 1974	DC, PSI, PSDI, PRI	230
Rumor V	14 March 1974–3 Oct. 1974	DC, PSI, PSDI	203
Moro IV	23 Nov. 1974–7 Jan. 1976	DC	410
Moro V	12 Feb. 1976–30 April 1976	DC	78

Government	Dates	Composition	Duration (in days)
7th legislature, 5 July 1976–2 April 1979 (general election: 20–21 June 1976)			
Andreotti III	29 July 1976 16 Jan. 1978	DC	536
Andreotti IV	11 March 1978–31 Jan. 1979	DC	326
Andreotti V	20 March 1979–31 March 1979	DC, PRI, PSDI	11
8th legislature, 20 June 1979–4 May 1983 (general election: 3 June 1979)			
Cossiga I	4 Aug. 1979–19 March 1980	DC, PLI, PSDI	228
Cossiga II	4 April 1980–27 Sep. 1980	DC, PSI, PRI	176
Forlani	18 Oct. 1980–26 May 1981	DC, PSI, PSDI, PRI	220
Spadolini I	28 June 1981–7 Aug. 1982	DC, PSI, PSDI, PRI, PLI	405
Spadolini II	23 Aug. 1982–13 Nov. 1982	DC, PSI, PSDI, PRI, PLI	82
Fanfani V	1 Dec. 1982–29 April 1983	DC, PSI, PSDI, PLI	149
9th legislature, 12 July 1983–28 April 1987 (general election: 26 June 1983)			
Craxi I	4 Aug. 1983–27 June 1986	DC, PSI, PSDI, PRI, PLI	1,058
Craxi II	1 Aug. 1986–3 March 1987	DC, PSI, PSDI, PRI, PLI	214
Fanfani VI	17 April 1987–28 April 1987	DC, independents	11
10th legislature, 2 July 1987–2 February 1992 (general election: 14 June 1987)			
Goria	28 July 1987–11 March 1988	DC, PSI, PSDI, PRI, PLI	227
De Mita	13 April 1988–19 May 1989	DC, PSI, PSDI, PRI, PLI	401
Andreotti VI	22 July 1989–29 March 1991	DC, PSI, PSDI, PRI, PLI	615
Andreotti VII	12 April 1991–24 April 1992	DC, PSI, PSDI, PLI	378
11th legislature, 23 April 1992–16 January 1994 (general election: 4 April 1992)			
Amato I	28 June 1992–22 April 1993	DC, PSI, PSDI, PLI	298
Ciampi	28 April 1993–16 April 1994	DC, PSI, PSDI, PLI	353

Source: adapted from Bull and Newell (2005: Table 3.1); Newell (2010a: Table 1.2).

role in policymaking was reactive. Whenever some event made a policy response necessary, they would seek to limit and channel their response in order to protect the interests they represented. Senior party leaders often remained outside government, delegating ministerial responsibilities to lesser figures as a means of distancing themselves from policy failures and keeping the Prime Minister and executive subordinate to the parties. As their names were associated with such a wide range of public institutions, the parties were blamed for their failures. Taking a reactive stance on policymaking from outside the government led their behaviour to be perceived as illegitimate interference in public affairs.

Meanwhile, the communist opposition was prevented from benefiting electorally thanks to the tendency for it to become caught up in the same processes of power-broking that attended the politics of clientelism. On the one hand, given the size of the PCI (as the representative of between one-quarter and one-third of the electorate), regime stability required that it be given *some* role in legislative policymaking—the solution that was found being the decentralization of decision-making to Parliament's permanent committees and giving the chairs of such committees to the PCI. On the other hand, government parties often sought to escape the consequences of indiscipline among their own followers by co-opting the support of the PCI in the passage of measures. If this enabled the party to obtain policy concessions and seek legitimacy by behaving 'respectably', then it led to public perceptions that instead of seeking to hold governments effectively to account, the party was often embroiled in a series of—frequently hidden—pacts with them, a state of affairs often referred to pejoratively as *consociativismo*.

Having reached the height of its power, with 34.4% of the vote in 1976, thereafter the PCI went into a process of slow decline, as did the parties of government. Long protected electorally by Catholicism, clientele politics and the strength of the subcultures, the parties were undermined by the rapid growth rates—5.3% per annum from1951–58, 6.6% from 1958–63, and 5.3% from 1963–69—of the post-war 'economic miracle'. This resulted in higher geographical and social mobility, growing secularization, an expansion of education and the mass media, rising living standards—all of which weakened affective party ties and fostered, with generational turnover, a more critical electorate whose dissatisfaction could be seen in declining turnouts (which fell at every election after 1976 from 93.4% to 82.7% in 1996); growing fragmentation (the number of parties represented in the Chamber of Deputies rose from nine to 14 between 1968 and 1987, the share of the vote obtained by the DC, the PSI and the PCI declining from over three-quarters in 1976 to less than one-half in 1992); and increasing electoral volatility. As measured by Pedersen's index (1979),[1] aggregate volatility 'rose from an average of 5.8 between the election pairs of 1953–58 and 1972–76 to an average of 9.1 between 1976–79 and 1987–92' (Newell, 2000: 20).

To some extent, the economic miracle was the product of wartime destruction, for if 'cities lay in ruins, if the railways and the road network were unserviceable, if there were shortages of basic consumer goods, then paradoxically, these very facts meant that the situation was rich with entrepreneurial possibilities' (Newell, 2019: 19). To some extent, the miracle was the product of American intervention. The Marshall Plan, motivated by the desire to revive the European economies so that they could import American goods and halt the spread of communism, provided more than US $1,400m. of development assistance between 1948 and 1952. When it became clear that the plan had failed to reduce the PCI to the size deemed appropriate for a democracy, US pressure on Italian governments of the 1950s to take measures against the party and the trade unions helped to ensure the competitiveness of Italian firms in international markets by raising productivity and depressing wages. Once again, the Cold War provides the key to understanding here. First, the Confederazione Generale Italiana del Lavoro (CGIL—Italian General Confederation of Labour) had been formed by agreement between the communists, socialists and the Christian Democrats in June 1944, but in 1950 it had split into the communist/socialist CGIL, the Catholic Confederazione Italiana Sindacati Lavoratori (Italian Confederation of Workers' Trade Unions) and the Social Democrat/republican Italian Labour Union (Unione Italiana del Lavoro). Second, if division reduced their bargaining power, and with it their membership, then their organizational dependence on the parties ensured that they were unable to remain free of the climate of political repression against the left in 1950s Italy:

> The dramatic confrontation in Korea heightened political divisions at home, with the Communists and Socialists depicted as the internal enemy and …. a serious risk that [they] and the CGIL would have their freedoms of organization and assembly limited by law.
> (Ginsborg, 1990: 187)

Finally, the emergence and development of the project for European integration, first through the European Coal and Steel Community, then through the European Economic Community was also an important driver of the miracle. Italy under De Gasperi (who was from the frontier region of Trentino and inspired by Catholic internationalism) was keen to be a part of the project from the start. This was because it offered a way back into international polite society after the war and the prospect of a solution to the structural problems of the Italian economy, especially mass unemployment and an underdeveloped south, problems Mussolini had sought to resolve by pursuing imperial ambitions (Ginsborg, 1990: 160). Since it created free trade, integration brought with it the opportunity for export-led growth through the Fordist production of consumer goods, such as fridges, washing machines and typewriters, in demand in advanced industrial countries with per capita incomes initially higher than those in Italy. Once underway, the processes of growth became self-generating. If, for example, rising incomes generated demand for new FIAT 500s and 600s—the symbols of the economic miracle—then car production in turn generated demand in a range of other sectors, from parts, to rubber, to steel, and so on. Workers in these industries required better roads, schools, housing and leisure facilities. Thus, in the space of a couple of decades, Italy went from being a largely agricultural and underdeveloped society to being one of the largest industrial economies in the world.

Such self-generating processes meant that the boom was concentrated in the richer north. Better infrastructural facilities there and the shorter distance from northern European export markets meant that new start-ups were more likely to be located there than in the south, which in turn would influence subsequent location decisions, and so on. Governments attempted to counter the negative implications of such processes for the age-old north–south divide through the Cassa per il Mezzogiorno (Fund for the South). Set up in 1950 to fund southern development first through infrastructural projects, and from 1961, also through industry, its activities together with those of the state holding company, IRI, brought into being a caste of Christian Democrat bosses in the south. These mediated between the state and local communities (Ginsborg, 1990: 162) and were an important expression of the party's exploitation of state power for the construction of consent. Their activities were not especially successful. The idea driving them was that investment in industrial plant, such as the steel works at Taranto, for example, would act as 'poles of attraction' for other activities and that in this way it would be possible to create a self-sustaining process of economic development and growing prosperity. However, many of the new plants were in large-scale capital-intensive industries, which therefore made little contribution to resolving the problem of southern unemployment and consequently did little to stimulate complementary activities. Hence, they became derided as 'cathedrals in the desert'. More significant for southern prosperity were the funds flowing in through the earnings remitted by southern emigrants: the most visible human symbols of the economic miracle and of the massive rural exodus and internal migrations it triggered. Internal migration affected over 9m. people between 1955 and 1970. At its height between 1960 and 1963 about 800,000 people a year moved from the south to the north. 'In Milan alone, the centre of the boom, 260,000 families arrived in the space of a decade, the equivalent to the addition of a city of 600,000 inhabitants' (Fiori, 1995: 28, my translation).

By bringing cultural homogenization and social fragmentation, the economic miracle resulted in a decline in the strength of voters' attachments to the traditional parties. If television, for instance, conveyed the sense of new possibilities beyond the local community, then it also isolated people as ownership of sets spread and the initial habit of watching it with others, in bars and cafés, died out. Urban living brought greater privacy. The expansion of car ownership brought greater mobility and a weakening of local attachments. For the PCI, therefore, there was a gradual decline in participation in party-sponsored activities such as those of the *case del popolo*, the local cultural and leisure centres that were one of the central pillars of the party's presence in the localities and of its strategy for the ideological incorporation of voters in the areas where it was strong. For the Christian Democrats there was the decline in church attendance and the weakening inclination to vote for the party even among those who continued to attend. For both parties there were the increasingly critical attitudes that came with higher levels of education and greater exposure to mass media. The economic miracle was, therefore, of profound significance for subsequent developments and for the transformation of the First Republic political system that was triggered, as we shall see in the following chapter, by the end of communism in 1989.

It was significant in another way. Rising living standards and the mass migrations helped to trigger what came to be known as *il Far West edilizio*, the uncontrolled and indiscriminate construction boom that took place in the wake of the miracle. On the one hand, people whose incomes doubled between 1952 and 1963 had more children and needed larger homes; the wealthy bought second homes by the sea. On the other hand, the new arrivals in the cities of the north confronted local authorities with inadequate town planning legislation with the need to provide schools, hospitals and other facilities to enable them to cope with the sudden influxes of people. Those with agricultural land became desperate to transfer it to builders knowing that a change of designation would increase its value several times over. It was by taking advantage of the construction boom that Silvio Berlusconi was able to make his first fortune and to lay the foundations for the making of a further, even greater, fortune through the construction, in the 1980s, of his television empire. Berlusconi and his role in politics were to mark, as we shall see, the principal line of division in the politics of what would be called the 'Second Republic'. So, it is to a discussion of the process of transition from the 'First' to this 'Second' Republic that we must turn in the chapter that follows.

Note

1 Measured as half the absolute sum of the differences in the percentage of the vote received by each competing party between successive pairs of elections.

3 Revolutions cultural, judicial and political

The decline and fall of the 'First Republic'

Since Italian politics was ideologically polarized around the perceived threat of communism, significant sectors of the governing class felt a sense of loyalty to the 1948 Constitution that was 'dual', or conditional, insofar as it competed with a sense of loyalty to the Atlantic Alliance. Consequently, with the complicity of the USA, they allowed themselves to become involved in the development of a range of covert arrangements and organizations, many with links to the far right. Through a series of illegal operations ranging from the Piano Solo coup plot of 1964, through to the Piazza Fontana bombing in 1969 and the Aldo Moro kidnapping in 1978, the arrangements provided the basis for the so-called strategy of tension—the creation of a climate of fear and disorder that would provoke calls for an authoritarian restoration of order, part of which would involve the organizational dismantling of the left. These developments coincided with a growing willingness on the part of ordinary citizens to question established values and practices—made apparent by the Second Vatican Council, the waves of worker and student protest in the late 1960s, the outcome of the divorce referendum in 1974—which in turn provided the basis for the emergence of new, left-libertarian ideologies and movements often willing to engage in radical, and sometimes in illegal forms of protest—such as occupations, unauthorized marches, 'proletarian shopping', rent strikes and so forth—and in extreme cases, violence. Combined with the developments associated with the strategy of tension, the result was to draw groups of the extreme left and right into frequent, sometimes daily, street clashes such that the 1970s came to be called *gli anni di piombo* (the years of lead).

Developments during these years, taking place as they did against the background of a rising spiral of violence, were directly related to the 'economic miracle' discussed in the previous chapter. First, the miracle worked in contradictory ways. On the one hand, its atomization and consumerism resulted in declining interest in politics, thus reducing the likelihood that some would take collective action against the established order—just as the Americans had hoped. On the other hand, its consumerist values were opposed by both dominant ideologies in Italian society: those of the church and the communists. Thus, it undermined the alliance of 1948 between Catholicism and the American model of consumer society; and it provided the basis for a revival of Marxist thinking among students rebelling against a malfunctioning university system, and among factory workers rebelling against long hours and low pay in conditions of full employment. Second, the spontaneous protest, through the university occupations of 1968 and on into the so-called hot autumn of trade union mobilization in 1969 had three important effects. First it gave rise to the Italian new left, expressed through the mushrooming of all kinds of revolutionary groups from Lotta Continua (Continuous Struggle) to Potere Operaio (Workers' Power) whose common element was that, while they were all anti-capitalist, as expressions of rebellion against authority they were also opposed to the established institutions of the left, especially the Partito Comunista Italiano (PCI—Italian Communist Party). Second, protest created popular pressure for reform. Some of it was exerted through the established trade union confederations, which sought to regain control of their rank and file members by first asserting a degree of autonomy of the political parties and then seeking to ride the tide of protest by making some of the demands their own. The result was a series of landmark reforms including legislation for the setting up of the regional authorities, for the popular referenda provided for by Article 75 of the Constitution, for the so-called Workers' Statute and for divorce. In these, the PCI played a minor and rather passive role, caught as it was between a desire to spearhead protest on the one hand and not to alienate the more moderate of its voters on the other. Third, the alarm created in establishment circles gave rise to the above-mentioned Piazza Fontana bombing of the Banca Nazionale dell'Agricoltura in Milan on 12 December 1969 costing the lives of 16 people and wounding 88 others. This was followed, on 28 May 1974, by a further far-right bombing in Brescia, killing eight, and yet another, on 4 August of the same year, on a train between Florence and Bologna, with 12 victims.

Against this background, the left moved in two opposite directions. On the one hand, in the early 1970s some among the revolutionary groups realized that, for all of the real cultural challenges they posed and for all of their street brawls with the far right, revolution was not going to happen any time soon. While for some this resulted in demoralization and inactivity, for others it led to the conclusion that revolution would have to be nurtured through a recourse to illegal action and violence. On the other hand, the PCI under Enrico Berlinguer (who had become General Secretary in March 1972) developed the theory of the 'historic compromise' according to which the strategy of tension could only be effectively countered if the party were willing to seek an alliance with the Democrazia Cristiana (DC—Christian Democrats) and assume a governing role on that basis. Even if the party were successful in winning a majority, any attempt to govern other than through the creation of a grand alliance of anti-fascist forces like the one that had characterized the period from 1944 to 1947 ran the risk of a repetition of the events that had recently taken place in Chile when a democratically elected government had been overthrown by an army coup.

The theory of the historic compromise was put into practice in the aftermath of the general election of 1976 when the PCI reached a historic high with 34.4% of the vote and came within four percentage points of the support won by the DC. Prior to the election, the DC had been rocked by scandals involving corrupt payments by petroleum refiners and by the Lockheed aircraft manufacturer. Eighteen-year-olds had been given the right to vote for the first time. It is likely that these events played a part in the PCI's advance, and that the advance could also be explained in part by the ongoing protests and by the welcome reception some voters gave to the prospect of bipartisan collaboration which the historic compromise opened up. Nevertheless, the smaller parties suffered significant retreats, and the DC and the PCI now commanded 73.1% of the vote between them: a result which drew them together in the formation of a government of national unity. On the one hand, street violence and economic instability led Berlinguer to believe that Italian democracy was in danger and needed defending. On the other hand, in the time-honoured tradition of *trasformismo* (turning enemies into allies), the DC was driven by the desire to do to the PCI what it had done to the Partito Socialista Italiano (PSI—Italian Socialist Party) in the 1960s (Ginsborg, 1990: 378). Thus it was that in August 1976 a DC government took office with the abstention of the opposition parties and the understanding that they were to be consulted on policy, followed by a further 'DC-only' government in March 1978, this time with PCI support.

By taking on this quasi-governing role, the PCI increasingly distanced itself from that part of its base that was to be found among the protest movements, leaving vacant political space that came increasingly to be filled by groups that were willing to deploy violence. This was dramatically symbolized by the kidnap and murder of the DC's Aldo Moro, architect of the national unity governments, by the Brigate Rosse (Red Brigades) in early 1978. They were convinced that the historic compromise represented a further edition of the betrayal, as they saw it, of the Resistance movement that had taken place in April 1944 when the PCI had joined the Badoglio Government, thereby obliging the remaining Comitato di Liberazione Nazionale (CLN—Committee for National Liberation) parties to follow suit. They saw themselves as the heirs of that movement. They were convinced that acts of violence would serve, by polarizing conflict, to foment revolution. The PCI in the effort to establish its credentials as a responsible party had by then become one of the most zealous defenders of the law-and-order measures put in place in this period to repress the acts of violence and was therefore among the firmest in opposing any negotiation to secure Moro's release.

The kidnapping represented the culmination of the years of lead and was in many respects a watershed. Although there were further killings in 1979 and 1980, successful police action against the BR and similar groups eventually put an end to violence. In 1979 the PCI withdrew its support from the Government disappointed with the meagre results in terms of reform its governing cooperation had yielded, and began a process of long-term decline at that year's election, losing 4%. From then on, it was every bit as isolated in opposition as it had been before the years of lead began. In the early 1970s the PSI had moved back into opposition but had been penalized at the 1976 election as the prospect that the PCI might then overtake the DC to become the largest party had led some of its supporters, along with some of those of the far-left groups, to converge on the PCI. Largely ignored by the communists in the construction of their alliance with the DC, and in danger, once again, of losing the distinctiveness of its appeal by too close an association with them, the PSI in the 1980s followed a radically independent path with anti-communism becoming one of its principal battle cries.

The 1980s were years of cultural change perhaps as profound as those associated with the economic miracle. In the first place, the economic difficulties of the previous decade eventually gave way to a new era of prosperity, 'which coincided with a decline in the political and social tensions of the 1970s and their associated activism and ideological debates, giving rise to what became known as the "retreat to the private sphere"' (Newell, 2019: 132). As elsewhere in the West, thanks partly to the beginnings of the decline in Fordist manufacturing and the shifts in the global division of labour that would be identified with globalization, there was a dramatic decline in industrial militancy. Political tensions revolved far less around themes of equality and the collective as during the years of lead, and more around themes of individual aspiration as expressed by the emergence of 'identity politics'. Associational involvements were less with organizations having all-encompassing world views, and more with single-issue and self-help groups. The emergence and growth of commercial television, driven especially by Silvio Berlusconi and providing entertainment as the means of maximizing advertising revenue, became both a cause and a reflection of the near hegemony eventually acquired by the values of hedonism and material acquisition.

Political developments reflected these changes. The PCI 'found its ideology and position as a mass party of workers under pressure as never before'.

> Its denunciation of 'the moral question', arising from illegitimate public–private links and associated instances of corruption, helped to nourish the spread of anti-political sentiments. It found itself and its Resistance symbols under virulent attack from a Socialist Party keen to avoid being cannibalised by the Christian Democrats to its right and the Communists to its left. With the collapse of the Berlin Wall and its aftermath, the Communists' commitment to ideas of political and social transformation, already fading, was finally extinguished, its ability to sustain any real counter-culture – around the values of social solidarity in opposition to the prevailing values of individual aspiration and material acquisition – long gone.
>
> (Newell, 2019: 133)

The socialists, meanwhile, rode the crest of a wave. The 1983 election provided the third confirmation in a row that the DC was no longer able to choose to between 'centrist' and 'centre-left' coalitions and the party suffered its most significant retreat since 1948. This had allowed PSI leader, Bettino Craxi, to capture the premiership. 'First Republic' prime ministers were usually weak figures, chosen by the governing party leaders to mediate their interests and without independent power bases of their own. Craxi was an exception to the rule. He had a power base as the leader of a party, which he ruled with an iron fist partly because, the PSI having become a vehicle for those seeking upward mobility often by means of doubtful legality, he was privy to numerous politically useful secrets. The parliamentary arithmetic meant that the DC was unable to retain office without him. With the advent of commercial television, he understood earlier than others that the future of acquiring and retaining power through party politics lay in the direction of a presidential and personalized style of permanent campaign; that is, using government as a means to support mobilization, while using support mobilization as an instrument of government. He thus anticipated future developments in Italian politics and used the premiership to establish a reputation for himself and his party for decisive and effective government, an attempt which was at least partially successful, for if nothing else he established a record for government longevity at 1,058 days.

In the longer term, the years from Craxi's advent initiated the disintegration of his own party and of his coalition allies in the decade to follow. Dependent on each other for their hold on office, the DC and the PSI were for that reason as much enemies as allies, each determined to pursue strategies that would free it from the tutelage of the other. For the PSI, this lay in the direction of an electoral reform that would establish a five percentage point representation threshold, thus obliging the smaller governing parties, the Partito Socialista Democratico Italiano (PSDI—Italian Social Democratic Party), the PRI and the PLI, to accept an electoral alliance under socialist leadership or else disappear. Combined with the PCI's ongoing decline, such a reform might eventually allow the PSI to pose as a credible centre-left alternative to the DC in a bipolar party system characterized by Westminster-type alternation in government. The DC, under its leader Ciriaco De Mita, on the other hand, championed the idea of a majority premium to be awarded in the event that there were parties willing to form an electoral coalition and in the event that they emerged as the largest coalition identified by the voters. Such a reform would also facilitate the emergence of bipolar party competition, helping the DC to re-establish itself as a modern conservative party and forcing the socialists to make up their minds whether they wanted to ally themselves with the DC or with the opposition PCI.

Public debate concerning these issues did two important things. First, it placed at the top of the political agenda institutional, and in particular, electoral reform as means of getting past what had come to be seen as a 'blocked' political system. That is, a system in which the impossibility of government alternation had come, almost as a matter of consensus, to be seen as the root cause of the system's evident dysfunctions, namely the lack of probity in public life and absence of the reforms needed to help the country to meet the challenges of the late 20th century. Even the PCI had come to favour electoral reform that would bring about bipolar, majoritarian democracy. Steeped as it was in the traditions of the historic compromise and the anti-fascist CLN before that, it had always favoured the principle of proportionality, which it took to be synonymous with democracy itself. However, this fell away with the failure of the historic compromise and the party's new strategy, from 1979, of posing as an alternative to the DC rather than as a potential ally. Second, the debates led to formation of a power-sharing arrangement (the so-called Craxi-Andreotti-Forlani agreement—CAF) between Craxi and two DC faction leaders, Giulio Andreotti and Arnaldo Forlani, who opposed De Mita in seeking to pursue an alternative strategy for overcoming the DC's dependence on the socialists. Whereas De Mita launched a ferocious attack on the socialists during the 1987 election campaign demanding that they choose between the DC and the PCI, Andreotti and Forlani sought to embrace the PSI in the distribution of political spoils on the assumption that this would eventually make it impossible for Craxi credibly to pose, independently, as a genuine reformist leader. With the outcome of the 1987 election (Table 3.1) revealing the failure of the De Mita strategy, and with his replacement as party secretary by Forlani in February 1989, the way was cleared for the full implementation of the CAF strategy which in the minds of its instigators, would be used to govern Italy until the next election.

The CAF axis was important because it was based on the parties' mutual vetoes. For this reason it was widely perceived as symbolizing a further degeneration in the quality of Italian democracy, and it made it clear that the possibility of majoritarian reform was stymied by the reform paradox. This is the paradox that the entities requiring reform are, precisely because their cooperation is required to realize it, the very entities that make it impossible. Consequently, the CAF was the catalyst for what became known as the 'referendum movement' spearheaded by the Christian Democrat Mario Segni, seeking, as described below, to break through the reform paradox by recourse to provisions of the Constitution's Article 75.

Before that, however, 1989 triggered another landmark event in the evolution of the Italian political system. Until the early 1980s—when successful dismantling of the remaining 'red' and 'black' 'terrorist' groups broke their escalation, and ideology became more pragmatic and less utopian, and protest more innovative but more peaceful—political violence was, as we have seen, the most spectacular manifestation of the fact that the main line of internal political division directly reflected that of the Cold War. As this was so, 1989 was a watershed year as much for Italy's domestic politics as it was for world politics generally.

Table 3.1 Elections to the Chamber of Deputies, 1987 and 1992

	1987 Votes %	Seats		1992 Votes %	Seats	Diff. Votes %	1987–92 Seats
DC	34.3	232		29.7	206	–4.6	–26
PSI	14.3	94		13.6	92	–0.7	–2
PRI	3.7	21		4.4	27	+0.7	+6
PSDI	3.0	17		2.7	16	–0.3	–1
PLI	2.1	11		2.8	17	+0.7	+6
MSI	5.9	35		5.4	34	–0.5	–1
PCI	26.6	177	PDS	16.1	107	–10.5	–70
DP	1.7	8	PRC	5.6	35	+3.9	+27
Greens	2.5	13		2.8	16	+0.3	+3
Pan-nella	2.6	13		1.2	7	–1.4	–6
Rete	--	–		1.9	12	+1.9	+12
League	0.5	1		8.7	55	+8.2	+54
Others	2.8	8		5.1	6	+2.3	–2
Total	100.0	630		100.0	630		

Source: author's compilation based on data available from the Ministry of the Interior at https://elezionistorico.interno.gov.it/.

The most immediate consequence of the collapse of the Berlin Wall was to provoke the 12 November 1989 announcement by PCI General Secretary, Achille Occhetto, that the party would transform itself into a non-communist party with a new name, the competing pressures on the party—the need to maintain its Leninist heritage as the basis of internal cohesion, and the need to attack it to acquire external legitimacy—having now come to a head. Occhetto's announcement set off a chain reaction that within five years had led to the disintegration of all the traditional governing parties and a transformation of the party system as a whole. First, it led to a major party split. At the 20th PCI congress, on 3 February 1991, a majority voted in favour of the proposal that the party should henceforth be called the Partito Demo-cratico della Sinistra (PDS—Democratic Party of the Left) and aban-don, as its symbol, the hammer and sickle in favour of the more innocuous oak tree. However, the pro-Soviet wing of the party and its anti-capitalist left broke away to form, together with the small liber-tarian left-wing party, Democrazia Proleteria (Proletarian Democracy), the Partito della Rifondazione Comunista (PRC—Party of Communist Refoundation). Second, it weakened support for the Christian Democrats and other governing parties by reducing the power of anti-communism as a basis on which to appeal for votes. Third, therefore, it assisted the fortunes of new parties such as the Lega Nord (LN—Northern League).

Founded in December 1989 by Umberto Bossi as a means of bring-ing together under one umbrella a number of northern regional autonomy leagues, the LN was a populist party whose initial following was built on the long-standing, and deep-seated economic and social disparities between northern and southern Italy. Preceding unification, the disparity had grown larger in the years that followed, since indus-trialization was a northern phenomenon, and this ensured that the economic distance with the south would be self-reinforcing thanks to external economies of scale. However, since unification had brought together north and south on terms of *formal* equality, then if the south did not progress—and if the corrosive effects of poverty on social soli-darity provided fertile terrain for organized crime, depressing inward investment in a vicious circle—it was easy for northerners to assume that the south's problems were due to some sort of congenital inferiority of the area's inhabitants.

Against this background, the League was able to exploit the feelings of relative deprivation that began to arise in the DC's north-eastern strongholds thanks to the post-war growth there of the so-called Third Italy based on small-scale enterprises whose prosperity owed much to the bonding social capital of localized industrial districts. Since the politics of clientelism mainly benefited the south while sustaining infrastructural inefficiencies damaging to small business, the League was able to exploit latent hostility to southerners as the basis of demands for northern autonomy by counter-posing northern interests to what it portrayed as a corrupt, party-dominated bureaucracy in far-away Rome. According to the League, inefficient public expenditure designed to underpin corrupt parties' southern support was financed by resources coming mainly from the north and by a growing public debt (up from 61.1% of GDP in 1981 to 100.9% in 1990). This threatened northern business by throwing a question mark over the ability of Italy to meet the convergence criteria for economic and monetary union set out in the Maastricht Treaty signed by European Union member states on 7 February 1992. Another issue that the League was able to exploit to reinforce the idea of northern interests under attack from outsiders was—for Italy—the relatively novel one of immigration. It was also able to pose as the authentic voice of ordinary northerners by adopting a simple, sometimes crude, linguistic style that deliberately broke with the cultured but opaque styles of the established parties (thereby exploiting latent resentments at the expropriation of power inevitably involved in the use of styles that were incomprehensible to the masses). As a centralized organisation under strong charismatic leadership, the League was able to protect itself against the potentially debilitating effects of factionalism.

The outcome of the 1992 general election (Table 3.1) was therefore widely dubbed as an 'earthquake'. Increasing its share of the northern vote from 2.6% to 17.3% the LN scored some of its most striking successes in DC strongholds. Meanwhile, the PDS, at its first electoral outing, won 16.1%—a vote share that was 10.5 percentage points below that of the PCI in 1987—while support for the DC fell below 30% for the first time in its history. The four parties then in government (the DC, the PSI, the Social Democrats and the Liberals) lost their overall majority of votes and only just retained (by 16 seats) their majority in the Camera dei Deputati (Chamber of Deputies).

A fourth development linked to the PCI's transformation was the great 'Tangentopoli' ('Bribesville') corruption scandal which first broke on 17 February just before the election—when the first of the defendants, Mario Chiesa, socialist head of a Milanese old people's home, was caught in the act of taking a bribe in exchange for the awarding of large public contracts—and rapidly gained momentum thereafter. The link had to do with the fact that resolution of the communist question completely altered the stakes involved in the actions of the judicial investigators responsible for the revelations. In the past, public prosecutors had often attempted to use their authority to pursue powerful figures in corruption cases as generational turnover had from round about the 1970s brought to the judiciary younger prosecutors who saw themselves as problem solvers keen to use their powers to moralize public life. However, politicians had been able to use informal relations of connivance with senior judicial personnel to curb the activities of excessively zealous junior officials through the judiciary's hierarchical structures. The parties' capacity to do this was decisively undermined by the ending of communism and the massive electoral setback for them that resulted. This made it clear to prosecutors that they had public opinion on their side, and that the parties had lost their former authority. All the principal actors involved—politicians, judicial personnel, entrepreneurs—were aware that for the first time in 45 years it was possible to pursue an effective anti-corruption drive, holding governing politicians properly to account, without running the risk that it would play into the hands of the communists who, at least since Enrico Berlinguer had become General Secretary in 1972, had made 'the moral question' one of their own great battle cries.

Apparently relatively restricted in the early post-war years, political corruption seems then to have spread to the point that by the end of the 1980s it had become systemic in significant areas of public life. Initially limited by the difficulties involved in establishing and maintaining the trust necessary to make corrupt transactions possible at all, it appears then to have spread in a self-generating way through a series of vicious circles. In some parts of the country there was the vicious circle between corruption and organized crime, with the latter using the threat of violence to underwrite corrupt transactions in exchange for immunity from the threat of prosecution. There was the vicious circle between clientelism and corruption with politicians using the proceeds of bribery to acquire clientele followings of a size necessary to enable them to acquire positions with even greater potential for the supply of corrupt favours, and so on. Finally, there was the vicious circle between corrupt transactions themselves such that the more they became the norm, the less willing entrepreneurs were to refuse to conform by reporting them, aware that, if they were under some pressure to observe the law, they were also under pressure to protect the interests of workers and shareholders and not least their own.

Consequently, once the initial revelations in the Tangentopoli affair had been made, with the naming of names obliging others to do the same, and they in turn to do likewise, a domino effect was set in motion, one that revealed massive networks of mutually beneficial linkages between politicians and entrepreneurs routinely involved in systematic processes of corrupt party funding. By the end of 1993 no fewer than 251 members of Parliament were under judicial investigation, including four former prime ministers, five ex-party leaders, and seven members of the cabinet.

The exposure of corruption on this scale resulted in complete disintegration of the traditional parties of government. During the 1970s and 1980s the parties had become increasingly dependent on corrupt forms of funding while facing mounting accumulated debts. Therefore, by reducing the amounts available from illegal sources of financing to just a trickle, the investigations pushed all the traditional parties fairly quickly towards bankruptcy. By effectively cutting off the flow of resources that provided the instrumental reasons for being a member of one of the governing parties, it left them vulnerable to organizational collapse—reflected in the dramatic decline in figures for party membership, which decreased from approximately 3,804,000 in 1991 to 1,330,000 in 1993. The governing parties suffered a haemorrhaging of support in the voting booths, with the downfall and humiliation of so many powerful figures who suffered from the revelations and thereby succeeded in delighting public opinion.

The sense of public outrage then provided the popular backing required by a range of cross-party groups and organizations that now tried to bring about a change in the electoral law for the Italian Parlamento (Parliament). The Constitution makes it possible to hold referenda on laws and parts of laws when they are requested by the signatures of at least half a million voters. Consequently, a number of reformers from across the political spectrum now managed to gather the signatures required to force the holding of a referendum to change the electoral law from one of proportional representation to one based largely on the first-past-the-post system. Since the Constitution only provides for referenda aimed at striking down unwanted existing laws, not ones aimed at proposing desired new laws, the tactic of reformers was to devise a referendum question asking voters to vote 'yes' to a proposal to delete the last 10 words of Article 17, Section 2 of Law 29/1948 as modified by Law 33/1992. The *practical* effect, in the event that voters did as they were asked, would be to leave the Senato della Repubblica (Senate of the Republic) with the single-member simple majority system for the distribution of 237 of its 315 seats. And since, as mentioned in Chapter 2 in this volume, the Senate and the Chamber of Deputies have co-equal legislative powers with governments required to retain the confidence of both, in turn the effect of that would be to create pressure for the passage of a corresponding law for the Chamber as the price of avoiding complete political paralysis.

Reformers were driven by the thought that such a system might put an end to the corrupt, inefficient administrations of the past, thanks to the political incentives on parties and voters under the first-past-the-post system. Such systems put parties close together on the ideological spectrum under pressure to reach stand-down arrangements across the constituencies in order to eliminate the possibility of parties further away on the political spectrum taking seats at their joint expense with less than 50% of the vote. Reformers thus thought that an altered electoral law would put parties under pressure to organize themselves into two broad electoral coalitions, one of the left and one of the right each competing for overall majorities. Voters would be under pressure, in each constituency, to confine their choices to the two best placed candidates, thus making it reasonable to expect that elections would result in an overall majority of parliamentary seats going to one or other of the coalitions and that, by virtue of the receipt of a popular mandate, and by virtue of competition from the opposition, the winning coalition's leader would enjoy sufficient authority to be able to impose discipline on the governing coalition and to use that discipline to ensure coherent policymaking as the means of maximizing the coalition's chances of being returned to office at the next election. Above all, the assumption of reformers was that under these circumstances, one would see the emergence of cleaner government, with governments making more efforts to tackle corruption as an important means of winning and retaining electoral support.

The referendum was held on 18 April 1993 and on a 77.1% turnout was won with 82.7% voting in favour of change. That such a large proportion of the electorate should turn out and such an overwhelming majority of them vote in favour of an obscure technical change was of no real surprise to anyone. This was because the vote took place at the height of the Tangentopoli scandal and was framed by the media as a vote of (no) confidence in the governing class in its entirety. A new electoral law was passed by Parliament in August. Thenceforth, three-quarters of the seats in both the Chamber of Deputies and the Senate would be distributed according to the simple plurality formula, and the remaining quarter proportionally. For elections to the Chamber of Deputies, the country would be divided into 26 multi-member constituencies and they in turn into 474 single-member colleges. The voter would have two votes: one for a choice of candidate in his/her college of residence, the other (for the remaining 155 seats) for the choice of a party list in his/her corresponding constituency. Valle d'Aosta would have one seat. For elections to the Senate, the 20 regions were to be divided into 237 single-member colleges. Votes, once cast, were then to be aggregated at the regional level and used for the proportional distribution of the region's share of the remaining 78 Senate seats.

With the parliament elected the previous year having been thoroughly delegitimized by the sheer number of its members caught up in the Tangentopoli affair, and with the results of the referendum now in, fresh elections were eventually called for 27 and 28 March 1994. In the meantime, the party system underwent a transformation that was interpreted by political commentators and media pundits as marking a shift from what they termed the 'First' to the 'Second' Republic. Obviously, this was not a regime change in the sense of a complete constitutional overhaul; however, the terminology was nevertheless meaningful insofar as it highlighted the fact that there was indeed a fundamental shift in the basic logic of party competition and government formation from the proportional and consensual to the majoritarian and competitive. On the one hand, the PCI's transformation removed the last of the pillars (Catholicism, clientelism, anti-communism) on which support for the DC and the traditional governing parties had traditionally rested, thus hastening their demise. On the other hand, the collapse of the DC and its role as a dam against the opposing extremes removed the hitherto insurmountable obstacle in the way of the Movimento Sociale Italiano (MSI—Italian Social Movement) finding partners in the construction of a conservative alliance to oppose the left. Thus, during the period between August 1993 and March 1994 the political forces reorganized themselves, coming together to form the two coalitions, of centre-right and centre-left, that would face each other at the general election.

On the centre-right, the coagulating force was Silvio Berlusconi and his new party, Forza Italia (FI), a 'personal party' (Calise, 2000) that was created, in the run-up to the election, by him and for him. The MSI—standing for national unity and a strong state able and willing to supply welfare benefits in the south where the party had its strongholds—and the LN—standing for northern autonomy and opposition to public assistance for the south—were unwilling to ally with each other. Both were, however, willing to ally with Berlusconi whose novelty, whose appeal to anti-political sentiments, whose promises of a break with the past and to do for Italy what he had done for himself were combined with vague expressions of social conservatism and neo-liberalism to make it seem likely that he would be very successful in mopping up the voters orphaned by the collapse of the former governing parties. For the MSI, the alliance offered legitimacy and the opportunity to emerge from the political ghetto. For the LN, it offered the opportunity of stand-down arrangements with a party which, given the overlap between its themes and those of the LN itself, would otherwise have been a very formidable competitor. Thus, the coalition of the centre-right in fact consisted of two alliances: the Polo delle Libertà (Freedom Alliance) bringing together FI and the LN in the north (where the MSI fielded its own candidates but was uncompetitive) and the Polo del Buon Governo (Alliance for Good Government) bringing together FI and the MSI in the south (where the LN was absent). On the other side of the left-right divide, what became known as I Progressisti (the Progressives) brought together the PDS, the PRC, the Greens and an assortment of former socialists and left-leaning former Christian Democrats. Finally, the centre of the political spectrum was occupied by a coalition known as the Patto per l'Italia (Pact for Italy) bringing together what remained of the DC, which now called itself the Partito Popolare Italiano (Italian People's Party), and the Patto Segni (Segni Pact) consisting of individuals and groups lined up behind former Christian Democrat, Mario Segni, who had been the main spearhead behind the 1993 referendum.

The reason why Berlusconi rather than any other businessman with more-or-less right-wing sympathies chose to take it upon himself to do the work needed to bring together in coalition the parties whose cooperation was required in order to fend off the left is understood once we know something of his background. Having made his fortune as a building contractor in the 1960s and 1970s, he used the capital he had acquired to extend into commercial television broadcasting after the emergence of a number of pirate stations from the mid-1970s sought to challenge the state monopoly. The economic miracle had created considerable pent-up demand for advertising only some of which could be satisfied by the state's Radiotelevisione Italiana (RAI) dominated as it was by powerful Catholic and communist sub-cultures with their opposition to unbridled capitalism and consumerism. After the Constitutional Court legalized the pirate stations (as long as they confined themselves to local broadcasting) in 1976, Berlusconi realized more clearly than his competitors (who took the opposite approach) that he could generate vast amounts of revenue by inserting advertising in copious quantities at the moments of greatest tension in films so that viewers would be induced to watch the advertisements as well as the films. Since large advertising revenues made it possible to pay for bigger names for his TV shows and thus attract larger audiences and still greater revenues in an upward spiral, Berlusconi was soon able to take over his commercial rivals. By developing his friendship with Bettino Craxi he then sought to assure himself of the political support he would need to block legislation on the assignment of frequencies and like matters that in other countries was used to regulate the broadcasting market and which in Italy threatened to obstruct his progress towards acquiring a monopoly on commercial broadcasting.

As Prime Minister from 1983 and with the power to dictate whether a governing coalition should stand or fall, Craxi was very well placed to assist Berlusconi and very happy to do so. The two men had an enormous amount in common on a personal level: unscrupulousness; an appreciation of decisiveness; virulent anti-communism; and a commitment to the accumulation of power and wealth for their own sakes. Their interests coincided. If Craxi could do political favours for

Berlusconi, Berlusconi could provide Craxi with access to commercial television, which the socialist could see represented the future of political campaigning.

Although Craxi was successful in his efforts to help his friend, by 1994 he had been cut down by Tangentopoli. Berlusconi's commercial empire was in difficulties and in need of financial consideration, on terms not normally offered, on the part of publicly owned banks in the orbit of the socialist party. There was a danger that an election victory for the parties of the left might result in legislation ending or restricting his broadcasting monopoly. There was a risk that the Tangentopoli investigations would begin to draw in some of his own companies. No longer able to rely on the political protection that had been essential to his empire's emergence and growth, he decided to take the place of his fallen protectors aware that he had both the financial resources and the skills to enable him to do so. By then he was a household name, one whose television networks, in selling products sold *lifestyles* and with them 'the vision of a new and better world ... a kind of utopian vision of infinite growth and infinite prosperity and well-being' (Stille, 2010: 76). And by making it possible, through the use of celebrities in advertising, for consumers to feel a greater sense of closeness to the celebrities with which they identified and desired contact, Berlusconi's television helped to enhance his *own* celebrity status. He understood more clearly than others that with the disappearance of the old ideological certainties after 1989, personality, charisma, celebrity, language and image counted for much more in the politics of the post-Cold War world than it had done in the past (ibid.: 192).

Berlusconi would dominate Italian politics for the next two decades such that, in much the same way that in British politics the period from 1979 to 1990 is often referred to as 'the Thatcher era', the period from 1994 to 2011 in Italian politics could legitimately be referred to as 'the Berlusconi era'. His control of power and use of hegemony enabled him to set his mark on this period (Gibelli, 2010: 7). The reason Berlusconi was able to dominate politics to such an extent is that it was he who brought financial and electoral resources (votes) to his party, not the other way round. His party, in turn, was the largest on the centre-right and therefore able to act as an effective 'coalition maker', that is, to dictate the terms on which negotiations for coalition formation in that area of the political spectrum would take place. As leader of the centre-right and as Prime Minister for much of the period, his position as owner of the country's three largest private television stations gave him a conflict of interests, which meant that his person and his role in politics were very rarely far from the top of the agenda of public discussion. They were the principal issues around which conflict between the two main coalitions competing for overall seat majorities mostly revolved. As one of Berlusconi's collaborators, Giuliano Urbani (2009), put it, 'to be on the centre right [meant] to support Berlusconi, to be on the centre left … to oppose him'. It is to the consequences of this domination that we turn our attention in the next chapter where we consider the politics of the 'Second Republic'.

4 The Berlusconi era

The politics of the 'Second Republic'

The outcome of the 1994 election (Table 4.1) was a victory for Berlusconi and the centre-right which obtained 366 seats in the Camera dei Deputati (Chamber of Deputies) and 155 in the Senato della Repubblica (Senate of the Republic) where it won the confirmatory vote of confidence thanks to the support of a handful of life senators, appointed by the President in accordance with Article 59 of the Constitution.[1]

Fundamental to Berlusconi's victory was the fact that by occupying a political space once inhabited by the traditional governing parties he provided a home for the voters orphaned by the parties' disintegration. His system of alliances was much more effective than that of his opponents who had been unable to include many of the Democrazia Cristiana's (DC—Christian Democrats) various 'successor parties', the most significant of which decided on an independent course that, as we have seen, prevented the left from extending its reach to the centre of the political spectrum. The sheer novelty of what Berlusconi was doing generated intense media interest, thus allowing him to dominate the election campaign, to set the terms of political debate and thereby place his opponents on the defensive most of the time. Finally, he was a far better communicator than they were. A single example, mentioned by Alexander Stille (2010: 190–91), is sufficient to establish this point. He was already known to the public as the owner of the football club AC Milan which had won the Italian Football Championship in 1988 before going on to win the UEFA Champions League, the UEFA Super Cup and the Intercontinental Cup in 1989, and again in 1990. Consequently, when his opponents asked him to defend his economic programme against charges that it would damage ordinary workers, he in turn asked them how many Intercontinental Cups they had won— thus inverting the class connotations of the exchange by making his opponents seem like arid university professors, while he, the billionaire,

Table 4.1 Election results 1994–2001 (Chamber of Deputies)

	1994					1996					2001				
	Single member seats		Proportional lists		Total seats	Single member seats		Proportional lists		Total seats	Single member seats		Proportional lists		Total seats
	% votes	No. of seats	% votes	No. of seats		% votes	No. of seats	% votes	No. of seats		% votes	No. of seats	% votes	No. of seats	
Coalitions:															
Ulivo/Progressisti	34.5	164	34.4	49	213	44.9	253	34.8	38	291	43.8	189	34.9	58	247
Casa/Popolo delle Libertà	46.4	302	42.9	64	366	40.3		42.1	77	246	45.4	282	49.5	86	368
Others:															
LN*	n.a.		n.a.			10.8	39	10.1	20	59	n.a		3.9	0	
PRC*	n.a.		n.a.			2.3	12	8.6	20	32	n.a.		5.0	11	11
Pact (1994 only)	0.8	4	15.7	42	46										
Valle d'Aosta		1			1		1			1		1			1

Source: Furlong (2002: Table 1.2).

Note: *The LN and the PRC were part of the main coalitions (the Popolo delle Libertà and the Progressisti, respectively) in 1994 and had full or partial electoral agreements with the coalitions of the centre-right and centre-left, respectively, in 2001.

came across as a winner whom the average worker and football supporter could understand and admire.

The victory was short-lived, however. The Lega Nord (LN—Northern League) was always a troublesome and undisciplined coalition partner, and it was aware that although, thanks to its alliance with Forza Italia (FI), its seat tally had increased dramatically, there had been a significant slippage of votes to Berlusconi's party, an indication that FI threatened the League's separate identity and distinct appeal. This was because both Berlusconi and the League's Umberto Bossi were populist politicians who in their different ways sought to issue a call to arms to ordinary Italians and small businesspeople against the oppression of the old political parties and against the economic and cultural elites that dominated the country. Thus, for Bossi, Berlusconi's activities represented an invasion of his own turf to some extent. Thanks to the stand-down arrangements in the single-member constituencies, the League's seat tally in the Chamber of Deputies rose from 55 to 117, while its share of the vote in absolute terms declined from 3,396,012 in 1992 to 3,235,248 in 1994. Meanwhile, 28% of those who had voted for the LN in 1992 switched to FI in 1994 (Newell, 2000: 115, Table 6.1). Tensions between the two were exacerbated by Berlusconi's failure to deliver on several promises, by his conflict of interests and by his clashes with the judiciary as allegations of corruption and false accounting came to light, prompting the entrepreneur to defend himself with loudly expressed claims that he was the victim of a communist-inspired judicial witch-hunt. In late 1994, as the annual finance bill was being discussed, the Government came under pressure from strikes and unprecedentedly large protests against proposals to reform the pensions system, leading to a dramatic fall in its approvals ratings. Together with the centre-left, the League presented a motion of no confidence. As it was backed by a clear majority, Berlusconi resigned as Prime Minister before the vote was taken, accusing his former ally of betrayal.

A technocratic government, none of whose members sat in the Parlamento (Parliament), under Berlusconi's former Minister of the Treasury, Lamberto Dini, was appointed in early 1995 with the support of LN and parties of the centre-left. Berlusconi himself referred to the episode as a 'bloodless coup' arguing that, as a result of the new electoral law, his coalition had received a direct mandate from the electorate and that since one of its components was no longer willing to respect it, the mandate should be passed back to the electorate through fresh elections. The claim that he had received a mandate directly from the electorate was both empirically incorrect (in no part of the country had voters been able to vote for or against the entire coalition of parties that went on to form a government) and without legal foundation. Constitutionally, voters elect legislatures not governments—whose legitimacy in turn derives not from election outcomes but from their enjoying the confidence of the legislature. President Scalfaro was unwilling to dissolve Parliament so soon after the previous election but he did not ignore the implications of the new electoral law. Declaring himself unable to sanction the formation of a new government composed of the LN and the parties that had lost the election of 1994, he asked Berlusconi to suggest a person 'acceptable to him who was capable of forming and leading a government for a relatively short, perhaps pre-defined period of time' (Pasquino, 1997: 41–42). Dini thus took office with the abstention of Berlusconi's party, announcing that his interim Government was an 'armistice government' designed to cool the tensions arising from the fall of the previous administration, and that it would resign once it had achieved a limited number of essential objectives. Fresh elections were therefore eventually called for 21 April 1996.

In the meantime, the forces opposed to Berlusconi's coalition underwent a significant process of reorganization, thus enabling them to compete with the centre-right much more effectively. On the one hand, the Partito Popolare Italiano (PPI—Italian People's Party) and the Patto Segni (Segni Pact)—chastened by the disproportion between vote and seat shares that had been the consequence of their decision to contest the 1994 election unaligned with the two main coalitions—now split between their left and right components. While the latter joined Berlusconi, the former joined the Partito Democratico della Sinistra (PDS—Democratic Party of the Left), the Greens and other assorted forces of former communist, socialist and left-leaning Christian Democratic extraction to form a new coalition, called L'Ulivo (the Olive Tree), under the mild-mannered economist and academic, and future President of the European Commission, Romano Prodi. Formation of L'Ulivo represented a recognition on the part of the coalition's mainstay, the PDS, that in order to be competitive with Berlusconi, first it would have to extend its system of alliances towards the centre and second, it would need to ensure that the coalition had a clearly designated leader and prime ministerial candidate—something that had been missing in 1994 but which the personalized style of competition inaugurated by bipolar competition and Berlusconi's political debut now made essential. The Partito della Rifondazione Comunista (PRC—Communist Refoundation Party) was excluded from the coalition but instead was given a free run, under the label

Progressisti, in a small number of constituencies in exchange for agreeing not to field candidates in the remainder. Thanks largely to this more efficient system of alliances, L'Ulivo won the 1996 election taking an overall majority in the Senate and a relative majority in the Chamber of Deputies where it was dependent upon the support of the 35 votes held by the PRC.

As for Berlusconi and the centre-right, although it put the entrepreneur out of office until 2001, the outcome was not a disaster for him. In terms of votes, his performance in 1996 compared favourably with his performance two years earlier (see Table 4.1). In the proportional arena, the parties of the centre-right actually performed better than those of L'Ulivo. Berlusconi was, however, unfortunate in being handicapped by two things that were largely beyond his control. The first was the lesser inclination of these parties' voters, when compared with voters for L'Ulivo's parties, to cast their vote in the majoritarian arena for their coalition's common candidate when the candidate was drawn from a party other than their most preferred one. It was this handicap that drove Berlusconi, in office after 2001, to use his majority to secure for the 2006 election the changed electoral law described below. He was handicapped too by the determination of Bossi to use the election to establish an unambiguously independent power base for his party by refusing an electoral alliance and campaigning on the extreme position of outright independence for the regions of the north. This decision was reflected in a new name for his party: Lega Nord per l'Indipendenza della Padania (Northern League for the Independence of Padania). Unless he demonstrated his distinctiveness, the slippage of votes from his party to FI seemed likely to continue. Although requiring the sacrifice of some parliamentary seats given the electoral system, the strategy was a great success in that it took the LN to a new high of over 10% of the vote.

Finally, the election outcome was not disastrous for Berlusconi because although he lost to L'Ulivo, in office the latter revealed itself quite incapable of passing the legislation Berlusconi most feared, namely legislation to curb his broadcasting monopoly and to deal adequately with his conflict of interests. In 1995 he won handsomely three popular referenda on issues related to the former—at least in part because the technical nature of the issues were not easy to understand and therefore easy for Berlusconi's television channels to reduce to the simple question: did voters want to retain their current viewing options or have them restricted? As for the latter issue, the centre-left was paralysed by the fear that any effective measures they took would inevitably be construed as an attack on Berlusconi personally. Thus, they would assist the entrepreneur 'in seeking to undermine the demo-cratic credentials of the centre left in the minds of ordinary citizens, many if not most of whom were unfamiliar with notions of conflicts of interest and therefore not at all moved by them' (Newell, 2019: 68). In addition, the centre-left was keen to get Berlusconi's cooperation in the workings of the cross-party Commisione parlamentare per le riforme costituzionali (known as the Bicamerale—Bicameral Commission for Constitutional Reform).

The appointment of the Commission was the first of what were the two most significant developments of the years between 1996 and 2001. Chaired by PDS spokesperson, Massimo D'Alema, the Bicamerale was responsible for drafting proposals for the revision of Part II (which sets out the institutional geography of the Republic) of the 1948 Constitu-tion. The significance of the Bicamerale was twofold. First, it repre-sented a widely held view that the transition from 'First' to 'Second' Republic was incomplete. The results of the transformation of the party system and the reform of the electoral law had been disappoint-ing, the government that had emerged from the 1994 election having been as short-lived and litigious as any seen under the 'First Republic'. More thoroughgoing institutional reform was therefore needed in order to deliver stable government and so complete the transition from the one regime to the other—as well as to deliver the federal reform of the state championed by the League and then accepted as common ground among most of the remaining parties (although 'federal' was never a term covering a precise set of widely shared objectives). Second, therefore, the collapse of the Bicamerale in June 1998, when Berlusconi withdrew support for it, confirmed the lessons of previous attempts at institutional reform, namely that it was subject to the reform paradox. And in collapsing, the Bicamerale placed itself in a long line of attempts at reform. Alongside a range of successful and unsuccessful attempts at reform of the electoral system, another attempt at con-stitutional overhaul would be made in 2006 and again in 2016. Driven by majoritarian conceptions of democracy and by the conviction that Italy was subject to a more or less permanent 'crisis of governability', the effect of all these efforts and of the political debates surrounding them was, arguably, to perpetuate in the political culture the populist and anti-political attitudes which would be of crucial importance to the rise of the MoVimento 5 Stelle (M5S—Five Star Movement) and the anti-immigrant League in the second decade of the new millennium (Floridia, 2018).

It is not entirely clear why Berlusconi withdrew his support, although his lack of genuine interest in institutional reform later became well known; and it was apparent that in order to have a chance of passing, the Bicamerale's proposals would require broad, cross-party support.[2] Its establishment therefore meant Parliament having to rely on different majorities for its activity—one for ordinary legislation, the other for defining new constitutional rules—so that from the outset it was at least doubtful that the latter would survive the tensions arising from the former. Once Berlusconi had withdrawn his support, the Bicamerale became in effect a dead letter since if he did not continue to support it then neither would the Alleanza Nazionale (AN—National Alliance). AN was the name the Movimento Sociale Italiano (Italian Social Movement: had adopted in 1994 in order to distance itself from its fascist past and thereby to consolidate the legitimacy it had acquired in the run-up to that year's election. It owed its new status to Berlusconi and was unwilling to jeopardize that by falling out with him over the Bicamerale.

The other significant development was the series of economic measures taken to enable Italy to adopt the single currency, the euro, which replaced the national currencies of those countries participating in Economic and Monetary Union in 1999. The euro notes and coins came into circulation on 1 January 2002. Reforms included an overhaul of public finances to reduce budget deficits and the level of public debt; administrative decentralization; privatization; and reform of the labour market. The reforms were significant for four reasons. First, they reflected the above-mentioned cultural assumption that Italy had a deep-seated problem of governability and that modernizing reforms were only possible when imposed on the political system through *force majeure* or the operation of some *vincolo esterno* (external constraint). Second, they therefore reflected political elites' (and indeed popular) convictions that European integration and thus membership of the single currency would help the country to overcome its 'backwardness'. Third, membership of the single currency, by bringing with it a transfer of sovereignty over monetary policy, removing from participating governments the power to set interest and exchange rates, significantly altered the terms on which future Italian administrations would be able to manage the economy. Most significantly of all, it considerably reduced Italian governments' room for manoeuvre in attempting to get to grips with comparatively very high levels of public debt. This, although it was successfully reduced as part of the efforts to qualify for the single currency (deemed essential for the competitiveness of Italian industry), began to grow again from 2004 (when it stood at just over 100% of gross domestic product) to reach a high of 135.3% in 2015. Fourth, therefore, since reductions in the debt in the context of single currency membership were very difficult to achieve without austerity measures, the reforms were significant in paving the way for the later spread of Euroscepticism among a public that had previously stood out, comparatively speaking, for its high levels of Europhilia.

Although widely perceived as significant achievements, pursuit of these economic reforms put a strain on L'Ulivo's relations with the PRC, with inability to reach agreement on the annual finance bill bringing about the fall of the Government at the end of 1998. Romano Prodi was replaced as Prime Minister by Massimo D'Alema at the head of a new centre-left government sustained in office by a number former PRC deputies—dissenting from the minority of their colleagues whose votes had allowed Prodi to fall and now breaking away to form the Partito dei Comunisti Italiani (PdCI—Party of Italian Communists)—and by a number of dissident parliamentarians who had originally been elected by the centre-right. The significance of this development was that it represented a reassertion of the power of the parties over the Prime Minister and the executive and therefore a return to a First Republic style of politics. This was visible in the number of governments that followed (see Table 4.2). D'Alema formed a second Government supported by a slightly different combination of forces in December 1999 and then in April 2000 resigned in the wake of the centre-left's disappointing performance in regional elections to make way for a Government under Giuliano Amato—and it was visible in the difficulties the governments faced in policymaking without intensive horse-trading among the constituent parties.

The centre-right's election victory in 2001—which owed much to the inability of the outgoing centre-left to capitalize on its governing achievements and overcome divisions to form an effective series of alliances, as well as Berlusconi's success in repairing his alliance with the League—confirmed that the main pivot around which Italian politics had come to revolve was Berlusconi himself. That is, it was Berlusconi the man—his private affairs, his role in politics and how he conducted himself—that had the highest profile in public debate and was the principal issue of contention between the two main coalitions. There were several aspects to this. It was very much bound up, first, with the reasons for which Berlusconi had gone into politics to begin with and, second, with the impact he had made having done so.

As we have seen, when he made his 1994 debut, through presenting himself as a novelty and a political outsider, Berlusconi was actually intimately acquainted with the world of politics and an active player in it, one who was aware that his business interests were threatened by the collapse of the governing parties on which he relied so heavily.

Table 4.2 Governments of the second republican period, 1994–2020

Government	Dates	Composition	Duration (in days)
12th legislature, 15 April 1994–16 February 1996 (general election: 27 March 1994)			
Berlusconi I	10 May 1994–22 Dec. 1994	FI, LN, AN, CCD, UDC	226
Dini	17 Jan. 1995–17 May 1996	Independents	486
13th legislature, 9 May 1996–9 March 2001 (general election: 21 April 1996)			
Prodi I	18 May 1996–9 Oct. 1998	PDS, PPI, Dini List, UD, Greens	876
D'Alema I	27 Oct. 1998–18 Dec. 1999	L'Ulivo, PdCI, UDEUR	423
D'Alema II	22 Dec. 1999–19 April 2000	DS, PPI, Democrats, UDEUR, PdCI, Greens, RI	119
Amato II	25 April 2000–11 June 2001	DS, PPI, Democratici, UDEUR, SDI, PdCI, Greens, RI, independents	398
14th legislature, 30 May 2001–27 April 2006 (general election: 13 May 2001)			
Berlusconi II	12 June 2001–23 April 2005	FI, AN, LN, CCD-CDU, independents	1,413
Berlusconi III	23 April 2005–17 May 2006		389
15th legislature, 28 April 2006–6 February 2008 (general election: 9 and 10 April 2006)			
Prodi II	17 May 2006–8 May 2008	DS, Margherita, PRC, PdCI, Greens, RnP, UDEUR, IdV	722
16th legislature, 29 April 2008–14 March 2013 (general election: 13 and 14 April 2008)			
Berlusconi IV	8 May 2008–16 Nov. 2011	PdL, LN	1,287
Monti	16 Nov 2011–28 April 2013	Independents	529
17th legislature, 15 March 2013–22 March 2018 (general election: 24 and 25 February 2013)			
Letta	28 April 2013–22 Feb 2014	PD, SC, UdC, NCD, PpI, GS, PdL/FI	300
Renzi	22 Feb. 2014–12 Dec. 2016	PD, NCD, UdC, SC, PSI, Demo. S, CD	1,024
Gentiloni	12 Dec. 2016–1 June 2018	PD, AP, CpE, PSI, CI, Demo. S	536
18th legislature, 23 March 2018–present day (general election: 4 March 2018)			
Conte I	1 June 2018–5 Sept. 2019	M5S, Lega, MAIE	461
Conte II	5 Sept. 2019 – in office	M5S, PD, IV, LeU, MAIE	

Source: adapted from Bull and Newell (2005: Table 3.1); Newell (2010a: Table 1.2).

Consequently, many of his claims to novelty were bogus. To claim that he was 'new' because he had not been a political leader previously, or that FI was 'new' because it had not existed before was to overlook the deals struck under Craxi's protection, the number of recycled old-party politicians within the ranks of FI and, arguably, to trade on voters' gullibility. That said, the party Berlusconi founded and made Italy's largest within a few weeks of its establishment was certainly a novelty in organizational terms. Light years away from the mass integration parties of old, it was a lightweight, 'personal' party (Calise, 2000). That is, it was not just a machine for the support of its leader, as parties were becoming generally, but one whose rules, organization, values and identity were entirely given and dictated by its founder. When combined with cross-national political and media developments that were turning politicians into celebrities, it meant that uniquely the party had little or nothing by way of an identity or profile that could be described apart from the personal qualities of the founder whose political career it was meant to advance. This made it seem unlikely that the party would survive the end of the political career of Berlusconi himself. It meant that Berlusconi's relations with his party and parliamentary followers were very similar to the relations between a monarch and his/her courtiers (Viroli, 2010). In other words, Berlusconi secured the loyalty of his followers largely through their material dependency and the distribution of favours to them such that, when they were elected to Parliament, they discovered—like Michele Caccavale (1997) who eventually left the party in disgust—that they had 'not got a leader but a boss' (quoted by Ginsborg, 2005: 69). Finally, all of this meant that it was not the party that brought votes to Berlusconi, but Berlusconi who brought votes to his party.

This had six major consequences for the nature of political competition generally in the Second Republic. First, it enabled the entrepreneur to act as the pivot around which the coalition of the centre-right was constructed—the indispensable element of coalition unity. Second, party system bipolarity and the success of the Berlusconi model necessarily drove the centre-left to imitate it, so that election campaigns increasingly became contests between two prime ministerial candidates. Consequently, in the 2001 election, with Prodi having by then departed for Brussels as head of the European Commission, the centre-left was led by Francesco Rutelli, chosen, precisely for his youthfulness and telegenic qualities, as the leader thought best able to go head-to-head with Berlusconi. However, Rutelli, unlike Berlusconi, was not the leader of his coalition's largest party and thus was promptly dispatched by the coalition's parties after Prodi was persuaded to return to Italian politics in 2005. Throughout the Second Republic, therefore, the centre-left had a larger number of weaker leaders than did the centre-right which had only one, namely Berlusconi. Third, thanks to his high profile and his legal difficulties, Berlusconi was driven, when back in office after 2001, to introduce a large number of *ad personam* laws—laws which were therefore emblematic of his conflict of interests and incidentally helped to ensure that corruption remained a significant problem in Italian public life. For example, as a defendant in the so-called SME trial (involving allegations that he had bribed judges to find in his favour in proceedings concerning the acquisition of shares in the Società Meridionale di Elettricità—SME) he had unsuccessfully sought the inadmissibility as evidence of a number of Swiss documents on grounds of formal irregularities. Consequently, in October 2001, just five months after that year's election, he got Parliament to pass a law in the matter of rogatory letters, to give legal underpinning to the inadmissibility case his lawyers had sought to make. A defendant in the All Iberian 2 trial involving allegations of false accounting, he secured legislation, which, by reducing the penalties for this offence, thereby reduced the time that would have to elapse before the statute of limitations kicked in and the time for which defendants could legally be held on remand.

Fourth, therefore, competition between the two main coalitions was always extremely polarized, with neither willing to accord the other legitimacy as a potentially governing actor. For Berlusconi, the centre-left coalition was an illegitimate contender for government because by insisting that he had a conflict of interests, it undermined his standing as a leader who had been supported by a majority in an election. By declining to criticize the judges and prosecutors involved in the legal proceedings against him, it upheld the actions of politically motivated people trying to inflict by judicial means the defeat on him they had been unable to inflict at the ballot box. For the centre-left, Berlusconi was, in the words of the famous *Economist* headline, published on the eve of the 2001 election, 'unfit to lead Italy' because he was intent on (ab)using public office for private gain. In relating to one another thus, the two sides reflected a very long-standing tradition in Italian politics for those in government to see their mission as being less about governing than about defending the state against the forces of opposition seen as usurpers. If this was clear in the case of the First Republic and its *conventio ad excludendum*, then it was a tradition extending back even to the period prior to the advent of fascism (Salvadori, 1994). The problem for the left from 1994 was that attacks on Berlusconi's role in politics failed to cut much ice with voters—which explains why, despite all the allegations of impropriety against him, he was able to remain very popular for so long. In this he was able to gain leverage from the widespread and deep-seated attitudes of cynicism towards public institutions among Italian citizens. Thus, if he claimed that he was the victim of a communist-inspired judicial witch-hunt then the claim would have resonance precisely because citizens were not convinced that public officials *could* be relied upon to behave impartially on the whole. And if he was accused by his opponents of feathering his own nest, then voters were likely to respond with a shrug—for isn't that what all politicians do?

Fifth, not far from being the only common denominator for the parties of the centre-left, opposition to Berlusconi was by that token a further source of division and weakness for them as they squabbled over how, and to what extent, to attack him. Sixth, the coalitions' polarization and their internal divisions helped to nurture and sustain levels of popular disaffection towards the parties that would be central to the later emergence of the M5S and the outcome of the landmark 2013 election considered in the chapter that follows.

The focus on *ad personam* legislation meant that by the end of the 14th legislature, Berlusconi did not have an especially illustrious policy record to defend. At the start of his term, the omens had seemed good. Though his government was a coalition, he was the leader of its largest party and had taken office at the head of a coalition present throughout the country and whose position was therefore directly legitimated by the electoral outcome. He could therefore expect, as a prime minister, to have rather more authority over his Cabinet and parliamentary majority than was usual in Italy—an expectation that was at least partially met insofar as his Government set the record for longevity: 1,413 days. So long as he remained popular, he would retain control of his coalition since his capacity to attract votes would mean that his allies needed him as much as he needed them. If this was the challenge, then meeting it was made difficult by two circumstances that were only partially under his control. First, to provide the tax cuts and all the other components of the 'new Italian miracle' that he had promised voters, he needed to achieve high levels of economic growth. He had famously appeared on television a few days before the 2001 election to sign a 'Contract with the Italian People' saying that he would withdraw from public life unless he failed to deliver on at least four of its five promises including tax cuts. However, given the constraints involved in membership of the euro, the cuts would not be possible without unpopular spending cuts in the absence of growth rates rather higher than the 1.06% per annum average he achieved during his premiership.[3] Thus, by the end of the legislature he had managed to force through fiscal adjustments that were just about large enough to enable him, without completely losing credibility, to declare that he done what he said he was going to do—but not without the loss of 75,000 public sector jobs to pay for it. Second, he could achieve nothing without managing his coalition. If this meant having to mediate the claims and demands of coalition partners which sought to represent competing interests—those of the north in the case of LN; those of the south in the case of AN and the Unione dei Democratici Cristiani e Democratici di Centro (UDC—Union of Christian and Centre Democrats)—then it was bound to disappoint voters who had been led to expect the stronger, more effective leadership he claimed to be able to provide as a successful billionaire who was lending his talents to politics.

The prospects for the forthcoming election did not therefore seem promising, inducing the Government, towards the end of 2005, to use its majority to change the electoral law and introduce what would become known as the 'Porcellum'.[4] In essence, elections to the Chamber of Deputies would take place according to the closed-list system of proportional representation, i.e. with the voter casting one vote for his/her preferred party; with voting taking place in 26 multi-member constituencies; with lower exclusion thresholds for lists fielded as parts of coalitions with more than 10%; and with a majority premium of 340 seats automatically assigned to the largest coalition. Similar arrangements were put in place for the Senate, with the main difference being that the majority premium was assigned region by region.

The Porcellum was designed to achieve three objectives of benefit to Berlusconi's coalition which since 2001 had adopted the name Casa delle Libertà (House of Freedoms). First, the 2001 election had confirmed the 1996 outcome in showing that centre right-voters were less 'summable' than centre-left voters. The centre-right won more votes in the proportional arena than in the majoritarian arena established by the 1993 electoral law, with the reverse being true for the centre-left. Henceforth, therefore, the voter would no longer have to make a choice of both party and coalition. Votes for a party would count automatically in favour of the coalition to which it belonged. Second, with voters no longer being forced to make a choice of coalition, the centre-right was under less pressure to campaign cohesively. In a context in which Berlusconi's shine was diminished, the new law reduced the significance of this for the electoral prospects of his allies, allowing each to present its own prime ministerial candidate and Berlusconi to campaign, as he did, almost as an opposition leader, claiming that his failure to achieve more than he had while in office was due to the obstruction of others. Given the narrowness of the centre-right's defeat, media commentators were more or less unanimous, in the aftermath, that this had been a very effective way of campaigning. It had allowed the entrepreneur to avoid having to take responsibility for his Government's record and, as he once again dominated the airwaves, he was able as usual to set the agenda and keep opponents on the back foot most of the time. Third, as the election outcome was, given the polling numbers, widely thought to be highly uncertain, the new law put parties under pressure to construct the most inclusive coalitions possible in order to maximize their chances of winning the premium. It would therefore ensure that even if the centre-right lost, the centre-left would find it difficult, if not impossible, to govern because it was the more unwieldy and divided of the two coalitions. Ultimately, this is what transpired. The centre-right fell short of victory by just 24,755 votes in the Chamber of Deputies contest (and actually had a vote, though not a seat, majority in the Senate) and the centre-left took office once more under Romano Prodi at the head of a nine-party coalition called L'Unione incorporating members of L'Ulivo and the PRC.

Precisely because they were clinched in the context of considerable internal tensions—and a majority so fragmented and narrow that powers of veto were possessed not only by single parties but also by individual senators—the 2006 Government's achievements were notable. They included action on tax evasion and public debt and a resumption of economic growth. But the Government's instability prevented it from drawing any benefit, in terms of popular support and approvals ratings, from its achievements. Obliged to be engaged constantly in internal mediation, Prodi was unable to engage in permanent campaigning. Individual parties' needs to survive and expand required attracting media attention—which, however, required confrontation and dissent. Thus, the Government's performance came to be framed, by the media, as 'catastrophic'. This, with its inevitable impact on popular ratings, effectively ensured that, by increasing the temptation of its components to abandon a sinking ship, prophesies of an early demise became self-fulfilling.

This in the end came about, in January 2008, at the hands of a small personal party—former Christian Democrat Clemente Mastella's Unione Democratica per l'Europa (UDEUR—Democratic Union for Europe)—whose actions once again illustrated the reform paradox. Campaigners were gathering the signatures for yet another referendum to reform the electoral law following attempts that had failed in 1999 and 2000 because turnout had not reached the required minimum threshold of 50%. They were driven by the awareness that while Italy had achieved party system bipolarity, it was an extremely fragmented polarity, with small parties retaining considerable blackmail power in the construction of electoral coalitions only then to go their own way, in Parliament, once the elections had been held. They therefore hoped to reduce fragmentation by removing the option available to parties to field lists as part of a coalition with other parties, and by striking down those clauses allowing attribution of the majority premium to the largest coalition. The result would thus be to reserve the premium to the largest single list, and automatically to raise the vote thresholds for all lists to 4% in the Chamber of Deputies and 8% in the Senate. The referendum could not be supported by the larger parties without risking the Government's survival. On the other hand, they could only head off the referendum through a reform which, by reducing fragmentation, also risked the defection of the smaller parties. Either way, for the latter, the only escape from the immediate threat to their survival appeared to be the Government's demise and a return to the polls—which would automatically lead to suspension of the referendum until a year following the election (when it might in any event fail, as indeed it did, for want of the minimum 50% turnout). Thus, Mastella withdrew his support for the Government, provoking its fall, a few days after the Constitutional Court's ruling that the campaigners' referendum questions were permissible.

   The general election of 13 and 14 April 2008 was fought against the background of a further reorganization of the principal components of the party system and of the two main coalitions. On the centre-left, efforts to overcome fragmentation and division had led, in 2001 and 2002, to the emergence of the Margherita (or 'Daisy') bringing together the PPI with two other formations of left-leaning but non-socialist extraction: Arturo Parisi's Democratici (Democrats) and Dini's Rinnovamento Italiano (Italian Renewal). In 1998 the PDS had sought, with partial success, to merge with four very small groupings of the left in pursuit of a social democratic project, with the new organization taking the name Democratici di Sinistra (DS—Left Democrats). In 2007 the Margherita and the DS merged to form the Partito Democratico (PD—Democratic Party) under the 52-year-old mayor of Rome, Walter Veltroni. Bringing together Catholics and former communists, it was a seemingly unlikely combination but one that was rooted in tradition—i.e. the tendency of the left of the old DC to be open to the idea of accommodation with the PCI, especially during 'the years of lead'. It was strongly desired by the activists and supporters of the two formations who were at least as strongly attached to the centre-left as a whole as they were to any of its component parties and wanted a more cohesive coalition as a means of defeating the much-loathed Berlusconi.

Believing that the outcome of the vote was a foregone conclusion, in view of the outgoing Government's approval ratings, Veltroni announced that the PD would contest the election without allies. First, he was aware that the unpopularity of the outgoing Government meant that re-proposing the centre-left coalition of two years earlier was politically unfeasible. Second, the PD had been created with what was referred to as 'a majoritarian vocation'. That is, its *raison d'être* was to monopolize the political space from the centre leftwards to enable it to take on Berlusconi's centre-right single-handedly. Third, the electoral system had created incentives that were the opposite of those it had created two years earlier when the outcome had been uncertain. In that context, the incentive had been to create the broadest coalition possible in order to maximize the chances of winning the majority premium. Now, the existence of exclusion thresholds and the fact that they were higher for non-aligned than for aligned forces meant that rejecting coalition with others made it likely that Veltroni would have to share the 45% of seats available for forces not winning the majority premium with fewer parties. Thus, he formed a coalition with just one other party (the small anti-corruption party, Italia dei Valori (IdV—Italy of Values) under the former 'Tangentopoli' prosecutor, Antonio di Pietro) leaving the PdCI, the Greens and the Sinistra Democratica (SD—Democratic Left) to agree to the PRC's terms for a separate alliance that become known as La Sinistra-l'Arcobaleno (SA—Rainbow Left).

Veltroni's appeal to potential SA voters to cast a *voto utile* (a 'useful vote') for the PD as the party with a better chance of defeating Berlusconi was widely understood as part of his strategy to monopolize the opposition to the centre-right by marginalizing the left, and in the latter respect it was highly successful. The SA failed to surmount the 4% exclusion threshold and thus to elect anyone—leaving Parliament, for the first time since the Second World War, without a single representative claiming to represent the socialist/communist traditions. This was yet another landmark. Essentially, the parties of the Italian left had been crushed by the experience of being in government from 2006. On the one hand, their decision to join the centre-left coalition seeking to unseat Berlusconi that year had been very much a 'coerced choice' (Newell, 2010b: 54) in the sense that a refusal to coalesce risked condemning them to electoral irrelevance. On the other hand, having joined the coalition, thereby enabling the latter (just) to remove the right from office, they found themselves having to grapple, in a government whose survival depended on the support of *every one* of its nine components, with the classic dilemma faced by *all* radical parties in such situations. That is, if they sought to exploit their indispensability as a means of advancing the causes of most concern to their core supporters, then, by appearing to put the survival of the government in jeopardy, they risked losing the support of more recently acquired but less strongly attached supporters. Moreover, if they bowed to the resulting pressures, they were exposed to the criticism of core supporters who would immediately accuse them of selling out. After two years of managing the dilemma as best they could, without parliamentary representation from 2008 'they risked being more or less ignored by the media; and, having suffered such a large cut in the financial resources available to them [thanks to the then system of public funding for political parties] their capacity to overcome this handicap was severely weakened' (ibid.: 65). And in fact, in the decade since then they have barely managed to achieve as much as 5% even if one includes in the calculations parties of the 'extreme' left (i.e. those parties seeking to revolutionize the institutions of the state rather than to participate in them).

On the centre-right, AN and FI were induced by Veltroni's announcement to come together to form the Popolo della Libertà (PdL—People of Freedom) and to agree to an alliance with the LN only. The leader of AN, Gianfranco Fini, believed himself to be the natural successor to Berlusconi as leader of the merged formation; both believed that the combined move would not jeopardize the coalition's lead over the centre-left (and with it the majority premium) and that there was therefore an opportunity to free it of the vetoes of the smaller centre-right groupings. Of these, only Pierferdinando Casini's Unione di Centro (Union of the Centre) and Daniela Santanchè's La Destra (the Right) decided on independence refusing, as the price of coalition membership, to take the PdL symbol in place of their own.

Simplification of the political supply resulted in a correspondingly dramatic reduction in fragmentation when, after a relatively low-key campaign (with the clouds of the international financial crisis on the horizon there were fewer of the Berlusconi theatricals than usual), the entrepreneur won his third election victory. The number of parliamentary groups decreased from 14 to six; the incoming government consisted of just two components—the PdL and the LN—so that it looked set to be the strongest in the history of republican Italy. The main parties of government and opposition shared over 70% of the vote and 78% of the seats between them—proportions higher than ever previously achieved since the war and well in line with the corresponding proportions for the other large European democracies. 'Fragmented bipolarity' seemed at last to have been overcome, and the Second Republic seemed at last to have come of age. Italian politics appeared to be on course towards a more positive future. However, from thereon things went rapidly downhill—as we shall see in the chapter that follows.

Notes

1 A copy of the Constitution, in English, is available on the Senate website at: www.senato.it/application/xmanager/projects/leg18/file/repository/relazioni/li breria/novita/XVII/COST_INGLESE.pdf.
2 For legal and political reasons: see Newell (2000: 139–43).
3 World Bank data available at: https://data.worldbank.org/indicator/NY. GDP.MKTP.KD.ZG?locations=IT&view=chart.
4 The term entered the lexicon thanks to the political scientist Giovanni Sartori who had famously referred to the 1993 law as the 'Mattarellum' after its principal sponsor, Sergio Mattarella. The 2005 law became known as the 'Porcellum' after its principal sponsor, Roberto Calderoli, referred to it as *una porcata*, translatable as 'a pig's breakfast' or 'a dirty trick'.

5 Decline of a celebrity and more
The end of the 'Second Republic'

The outcome of the 2008 election was dramatic. The centre-right coalition led by Silvio Berlusconi won with 46.3% of the vote, putting him almost 10 percentage points in front of his nearest rival, Walter Veltroni, whose centre-left coalition took 37.5%. Thanks to this and to the significant reduction in party system fragmentation mentioned at the end of the preceding chapter, there was a widespread feeling in the immediate aftermath that what had just taken place had brought to a head that process of political change initiated with the birth of the Second Republic in the 1990s, and thus that it represented a genuine watershed.

For one thing, the incoming Government looked set to be a very strong one by Italian standards and it came as little or no surprise to anyone that the process by which the Government was formed was very quick. The Constitution vests the task of appointing the Prime Minister in the President of the Republic, and if appointments prior to the party system upheavals of the early 1990s had often required lengthy discussions and negotiations with the political parties, in 2008 there was never any doubt about the identity of the person to whom the appointment would go. The President is also responsible for appointing members of the Government on the advice of the Prime Minister-designate once he (they have all been male so far) has succeeded in reaching agreement with the relevant parties; yet, famously, Berlusconi is said to have gone into the customary post-election meeting with the President with his list of ministers already prepared. The number of days separating the date of the election and the date the new Government formally assumed office was thus the shortest in the history of the Republic: 24, compared with a post-war average of 46.

In the second place, it seemed likely that Parlamento (Parliament) would witness the emergence of more clear-cut governing and opposition roles. Politics since the Second World War had of course always been based on the assumption that at any given moment certain parties were part of the government and that the remainder were part of the opposition. However, high fragmentation meant that the legislative behaviour of the parliamentary groups had often belied such simple conceptualizations. Most proposals that made it onto the statute book did so thanks to ample majorities drawn from across the governing/opposition divide (Capano and Giuliani, 2001; Newell, 2006); and there was no formal recognition in Parliament's standing orders of an official opposition. Now there was a governing majority staffed by just two groups and a similar simplification among the ranks of the non-governing parties. The emergence of a 'shadow Cabinet' drawn from the largest opposition party, despite its lack of formal, institutional recognition, allowed the work of each Cabinet minister to be shadowed by a politician potentially able to act as a spokesperson for the non-governing parties collectively and thus facilitate more straightforward patterns of interaction between more cohesive majority and minority coalitions.

Finally, it seemed that what had come to be called 'the never-ending transition'—the process of institutional and constitutional overhaul that appeared to have been set in motion by the political upheavals of the early 1990s but was obstructed by partisan veto players (Tsebelis, 2002) all wanting change, but changes going in contrasting directions—now stood a good chance of being concluded. Provided that they could agree among themselves, the Popolo della Libertà (PdL—People of Freedom) and the Partito Democratico (PD—Democratic Party) had many more votes than required by the Constitution to enable them to effect change with the certainty that it would not be vulnerable to repeal.[1] During the election campaign Berlusconi and Veltroni had abandoned a style of competition—reciprocal denials of the claims of the other to legitimacy—that had hitherto contributed significantly to rendering institutional reform intractable. Both men had clear incentives to reach, with the other, the necessary agreement on reform: successful reform arguably offered the opportunity of a place in Italian political history as the fathers of a new constitutional settlement, something that seemed likely to be especially attractive to the ageing Berlusconi, who was reputed to want to crown his career at the end of his term as Prime Minister with election to the presidency.

In short, there was a feeling in the immediate aftermath of the 2008 election that what had taken place would very likely come to signify the start of a new era in Italian politics—one of improved governance, Westminster-style politics, and institutional overhaul. When in August 2008 the American magazine, *Newsweek*, published an article praising

Berlusconi for having, as it put it, 'brought order to chaotic Italy' (Barigazzi, 2008) it reflected this public mood. Disappointment in all three areas followed not long afterwards.

First, the Government's hold on office was weakened when, in 2010, a bitter public row took place between Berlusconi and Gianfranco Fini, prompting the latter to leave the PdL, taking with him 33 deputies and 10 senators to form the new Futuro e Libertà per l'Italia (FLI—Future and Freedom for Italy). The dispute arose from policy disagreements and a divergence of view concerning the character of the PdL and its future direction. The two politicians disagreed about immigration and the Government's use of emergency decree-making. Fini was unhappy that the PdL had turned out to be just another 'personal party' without any ideological profile or image clearly separate from that of Berlusconi himself. This was a significant weakness, since it left few alternative means of retaining voter loyalty in the event that some external difficulty began to tarnish the leader's image, a state of affairs that had reinforced Fini's aspirations to succeed the entrepreneur who was already well into his seventies. Fini aspired to be part of a modern national party, committed to law and order and upholding the Constitution, which would give Italy the strong, moderate conservative party it had always lacked. Fini's departure meant that on 14 December the Government survived by just three votes a confidence motion instigated by FLI and supported by the parties of the centre and the centre-left. Moreover, the growing tensions between Berlusconi and Fini had heightened the level of factionalism within the PdL, which both undermined Berlusconi's authority and fomented indiscipline and organizational weakness on the ground—making, in turn, more likely the kind of financial irregularity of which a succession of party officials and locally elected representatives were now accused. To all this was added the seemingly endless series of allegations concerning the Prime Minister's sexual conduct, which began on 28 April 2009 and rumbled on into 2010 and 2011. Although the extent to which the allegations amounted to a genuine 'scandal' was unclear (given that Berlusconi already had a colourful public persona), they did appear to threaten his reputation, and certainly threw a question mark over his credibility as a prime minister. Finally, therefore, the Government was perceived as being inactive in important areas of policymaking, a widely held assumption being that this was due to the Prime Minister's legislative priorities being focused on areas such as the administration of justice that were more closely connected to his personal financial interests. Some 10 months after the election, the Government had managed to get 68.6% of its bills approved compared to a post-war average of 73.7% and 64.3% for the corresponding period following the start of the preceding legislature, even though the government in office at that time was litigious and its parliamentary support base, in the Senate at least, was fragile (Newell, 2009). Thus, while the Government's approval ratings stood at 53% in May 2008, by the end of 2010 they had sunk to 24% and by September of 2011 were down to just 19%.

With regard to the emergence of a more clearly defined role for the opposition, a study by Russo and Verzichelli (2009) showed that seven months after the start of the new legislature, shadow Cabinet ministers had made little use of the procedures by which deputies and senators can ask questions of ministers, so did not appear to be actually challenging their opponents in public. Nor were the opposition parties operating in alliance with each other, with only 27 questions (less than 10%) having been asked by parliamentarians of one group with the support of any of the other opposition groups. The authors were thus led to conclude that 'competition rather than cooperation' seemed to be the key to understanding relations among the opposition parties.

The conclusion was unsurprising. Ever since the election, the PD's main opposition partner, Italia dei Valori (IdV—Italy of Values) led by former 'Tangentopoli' prosecutor, Antonio di Pietro, a party whose *raison d'être* was probity in public life and whose anti-Berlusconi rhetoric was therefore unremitting, had been hard at work outflanking the PD by seeking to consolidate its image as being a far more consistent and aggressive, that is, *resolute*, opponent of the incumbent Government and Prime Minister than PD leader, Walter Veltroni, often attacking the latter for timidity in the process. Thanks to its divisions, the centre-left opposition was unable to capitalize on the Government's difficulties, with voting intention data showing that between November 2009 and December 2011 support for the PD increased slightly, from 27.9% to 28.5%, while that for IdV declined slightly, from 7.7% to 7.0%. On the one hand, IdV fished in the same pool of voters as the PD, so advance for one tended to come at the expense of the other without much advance for the two together. Moreover, IdV was a populist party whose leader's periodic outbursts against the improprieties of Berlusconi sometimes embarrassed the PD, thus making it more difficult for the party to build alliances towards the centre of the political spectrum—a strategy, which, notwithstanding the PD's 'majoritarian vocation' seemed essential if at a future election the centre-right was to be removed from power. On the other hand, the PD could not afford to ignore either its left flank or IdV, with the result that it suffered from an image of indecisiveness, unable to convey the sense that it represented a convincing and attractive alternative to the government in office.

Finally, the prospects for a swift conclusion to the never-ending transition were soon ended as, not long after the election, Berlusconi's conflict of interests rose once more to the top of the political agenda. An initial boost to the prospects had come in May when, with Veltroni insisting that opposition to the Government had to be 'constructive', Berlusconi seemed to reciprocate by insisting that the two should hold a meeting to initiate a dialogue that would result in agreed-upon changes to the rules of the game (a meeting that did in fact take place on 16 May 2008, just one day after the Government received the second of its two obligatory votes of confidence in Parliament). However, the conflict of interests meant that there were inherent tensions between dialogue on constitutional reform, and the requirements of effective opposition. On the one hand, the notably restrained nature of Veltroni's response to the issues involved[2] was insufficient to prevent Berlusconi, in July, casting doubt on the prospects for dialogue and accusing the PD 'of having brought into Parliament extremist and punitive fringes' (Montanari, 2008). On the other hand, the PD leader's attempts to keep hopes of dialogue alive were unable to satisfy radical critics who argued that the effect would be to prevent the opposition from keeping the Government accountable—as earlier attempts at cooperation had suggested would happen.[3] Moreover, the attempts risked weakening the PD, as polls suggested. Thus, if in June 51% of those who had voted for the centre-left in April judged the opposition to be conducting itself in a 'balanced' way, 41% felt that it was 'too docile' (Mannheimer, 2008).

It was against this background that the eurozone crisis gathered pace, leading to Berlusconi's resignation on 12 November 2011. The international financial meltdown, originating in the early years of the 21st century in the US sub-prime mortgage crisis, brought a slowdown in growth rates worldwide, making it more difficult for the Greek Government to service its public debt—leaving investors to demand higher interest rates and the Greeks unable to deal with the problem through devaluation because the country was a member of the eurozone. With the European Union (EU), the International Monetary Fund and the European Central Bank struggling to contain the risk of Greek debt and interest rates spiralling out of control, investors began to worry about Italy—whose public debt in 2011 stood at about 120% of gross domestic product and was second in size only to that of Greece—aware that the country's capacity to deal with the problem was compromised by a range of structural problems with its economy, including public services inefficiencies. In mid-2011 interest rates on Italian bonds began to rise, with the prospect that rising rates might bring about that very un-sustainability of the debt that was driving rates up in the first place.

The crisis was potentially the more serious for being one in which not only Italy but the whole of the international community had a stake. First, there was the risk of financial contagion. Much of Italy's debt was owned by French banks which, in the case of an Italian default, would put the French banking system and economy under considerable pressure which would in turn affect France's creditors, and so on. Second, the crisis was perceived as one that affected the eurozone as a whole. On the one hand, if the stronger countries refused to support those in difficulty, then the risk was that the situation might spin out of control with growing debt and spiralling interest rates on government bonds leading eventually to the weaker countries' insolvency. On the other hand, to the extent that attempts to avoid such a scenario required bailouts and austerity measures, there was the likelihood and the actuality of resistance to austerity in the debtor countries, and popular resentment against financial aid packages in the creditor countries—with all that that implied for the political project of European integration

The Prime Minister reacted by suggested that there was nothing to worry about, arguing on 3 August in a speech apparently intended to calm the markets that Italy's banks were 'liquid, solvent, and [had] easily passed the European stress tests' and that the country had 'also seen significant signs of recovery despite the uncertainty of the economic situation'. This put him at odds with his Minister of Finance, Giulio Tremonti, who unlike Berlusconi—concerned to win back declining popularity—wanted severe spending cuts. The upshot was a July budget that satisfied no one—cuts of €47,000m. were proposed that sought to eliminate the budget deficit by 2014; however, most of them were postponed to 2013 and 2014—and was read as a sign of the executive's inability to take decisive measures.

The President of the Republic, Giorgio Napolitano, stepped in urging the Government and the opposition to take concerted action to deal with the crisis so that, when the budget was duly passed with the support of the opposition, it looked as though Berlusconi had been sidelined by the President. With German Chancellor, Angela Merkel, and French President, Nicolas Sarkozy, making strong hints from August that a solution to the Italian debt crisis required a change of government, thereby feeding speculation that Berlusconi's political career was drawing to a close, his followers began to desert him. Votes on 10 October and 8 November suggested that Berlusconi was no longer able to command the confidence of a majority in Parliament. Thus, facing the prospect of defeat in a probable confidence motion, Berlusconi made a last-ditch attempt to save his position by promising to resign once a package of measures agreed with the EU on 26 October had been passed—calculating that by then the measures would have calmed the markets, thereby enabling him to rebuild his majority and not have to resign after all. But he was outmanoeuvred by the President who issued a statement reiterating Berlusconi's promise (thus effectively locking him into it) and declaring that presidential consultations to find a solution to the government crisis consequential upon Berlusconi's resignation would begin immediately. The event was highly curious politically and constitutionally; for, in effect, Berlusconi had been dismissed by the President—leading commentators to suggest that the weakness of the parties, revealed by their evident inability to provide firm leadership in a crisis, had resulted in a corresponding increase in presidential authority that gave Italy a de facto semi-presidential system of government.

This impression was reinforced by the Government appointed to replace Berlusconi's—the technocratic government under renowned economics professor and former EU commissioner Mario Monti—which owed its authority entirely to that of the President and was now supported in the confirmatory confidence vote by both the PdL and the PD aware that in the international crisis situation they could hardly do otherwise (and aware too that a period of non-party government might enable them to avoid having to take public responsibility, in a later election, for austerity measures).

The advent of the Monti Government thus revealed two important features of the Italian political system in the early 21st century, one long-standing, the other relatively new. The long-standing one concerned the role of the President as set out in the 1948 Constitution. Although the founding document says rather little about the Presidency, and although it refrains from conferring on the institution the powers typical of presidential systems of government, in its relative silence it confirms that the functions of the President are *more* than merely ceremonial. The President's powers (of which the main ones are appointing the government, dissolving Parliament and promulgating laws) are outlined in just three articles of the Constitution: Articles 87–89. The Constituent Assembly wanted presidents to coordinate and to moderate the activities of political actors (ensuring that the interactions through which acts having the force of law were pursued took place in a manner consistent with the Constitution), and therefore to *govern* in that sense even while remaining *super partes*. For this reason, the roles and responsibilities of the President were difficult to articulate in legal terms and it was precisely because of the relative lack of qualification and specification of the presidential powers in the constitutional text that the President was able to play such a crucial stabilizing role during the 2011 crisis. The scope for presidential decision-making depends on the multiple power resources of other relevant political actors, especially the parties, so that the latitude presidents enjoy can be likened to an accordion, the bellows of which remain closed when the parties are powerful and determined, but which is played to its fullest extent when they are not.[4] Second, therefore, the appointment of Monti confirmed that by the end of 2011 the Italian parties had reached a point at which they were chronically weak. That is, as organizations existing outside Parliament and the public institutions, they had, to a significant extent if not completely, atrophied, and their distinct ideological profiles had faded as they had increasingly become 'personalized' entities, vehicles for the pursuit of the ambitions of this or that leader of the moment. As a consequence, they lacked the authority needed to mobilize public opinion in the way that would have enabled them to provide the firm leadership that was required in 2011. It was for this reason that they were obliged, in essence, to step aside and play a supporting role to the new emergency government that now took office.

The incoming Government promised an integrated package of budget discipline, the credibility of which relied on growth that in turn required measures considered to embody fairness. By the end of February 2012 there had been measures to increase taxes and to reduce spending, as well as provisions designed to increase market competition in various sectors (such as the professions) and to improve infrastructural facilities (including the establishment of a fast-track court for the resolution of business disputes). The gross yield on 10-year Italian government bonds had fallen to 4.95%—about the level it had been before the onset of the Italian debt crisis. The Government's domestic and international prestige enabled it to pass measures which, in other circumstances, would probably have been unacceptable to both of the two main parties.

Meanwhile, the political parties were suffering further reverses to what remained of their authority and prestige. The PD lurched from one crisis to another. Having secured a triumphal election as the party's first secretary with 75% of the vote in an election extending beyond the members to include party supporters in the wider electorate, by the beginning of 2009 Walter Veltroni's leadership had been completely undermined by a series of poor electoral performances.

Regional elections in Abruzzo in December 2008 had seen support for the PD decline to 19.6% from the 35.4% its constituent parties had won there in the regional elections of 2005. The Sardinian regional election in February 2009 saw its support decline from the 24.1% won by its constituent parties in the regional election of 2004 to 21.5%, thus provoking Veltroni's resignation. The election outcomes seemed to be attributable to the fact that the party lacked an ideological profile that voters could easily identify or relate to. It seemed unsurprising that the party lacked such a profile, since Veltroni had based his leadership precisely on the idea that the familiar traditions, post-communist and former Christian Democrat, already rapidly fading, could coexist—and in any case needed, in a post-ideological world, to be overcome—in a *partito leggero*, i.e. a party with a slimmed-down extra-parliamentary organization and firm leadership from the top. The problem was that nothing was found to replace the old traditions as a source of ideals and principles that would give the party its *raison d'être* and make people want to join it. Moreover, by placing the decision about the identity of the leader *outside* the party (through what were popularly, if inaccurately, referred to as 'primary elections') the PD's statute turned it into a kind of plebiscitary democracy, undermining the organizations of the 'party on the ground' (Katz and Mair, 1993) as forums for discussion and deliberation, and so turning them, as bodies whose membership was linked to the fortunes of the leadership candidates, into assemblies for the *ratification* of decisions as opposed to ones able to enforce effective *accountability* of the leader (Floridia, 2019, ch. 2).

Other parties faced even more severe difficulties. In early April 2012 the leader of the Lega Nord (LN—Northern League) Umberto Bossi and his close followers were implicated in allegations of false accounting and misuse of money made available under the regulations providing for the public funding of political parties—a devastating blow to a party at the core of whose image lay the Spartan purity of its activists (Cremonesi, 2012) and whose stated purpose from the start had been precisely the protection of northerners against corrupt parties based in Rome. The revelations conveyed the message that, despite its claims to the contrary, the LN was in reality just a more or less corrupt party like all the others, one whose leaders were clearly unwilling to share the hardships, at a time of austerity, that were having to be faced by the ordinary hard-working northerners the party claimed to represent.

In municipal elections in May 2012, involving about one-fifth of the Italian electorate, support for the centre-right collapsed, while the centre-left took control of 96 of the 168 municipalities of more than 15,000 inhabitants (up from 56) but only because its support base had declined by a somewhat smaller proportion than that of its adversaries. A new, populist, formation, the anti-establishment and anti-corruption MoVimento 5 Stelle (M5S—Five Star Movement), had spectacular success, securing control of four municipalities, including Parma, adding to the impression that citizens had been voting not just for a change of incumbents, but for a change in the very mode of conduct of political life.

The M5S had been founded by the comedian Beppe Grillo who already had a public profile as an interpreter of anti-political sentiments. In 1986 he had famously embarrassed the Partito Socialista Italiano (Italian Socialist Party) on live television with a joke about the party's shaky grasp of the principles of public probity and which had led to the drying up of future offers of contracts from the public broadcaster. In 2005, then, he had issued an invitation to the followers of his blog to use MeetUp.com to get together and transform online discussion into a movement for change. Thanks to the success of this initiative several groups were able to assemble in 2007 to agree on a number of principles for the creation of a network of non-party lists based on the principles of direct participatory democracy and were considerably strengthened by the subsequent success of large rallies organized by Grillo in several cities in September and in April 2008. Called 'V Days', where the letter 'v' stood for *vafanculo!* (or 'fuck off!'), the rallies were designed to enable the gathering of the signatures necessary to promote a range of reforms through recourse to Article 71 the Constitution (making possible the introduction of legislative proposals by popular initiative) as well as Article 75 (for the holding of referenda). What gave the rallies their political power was that they were organized and publicized, without the support of the mainstream media, entirely through the horizontal dissemination of information through the internet (Pepe and di Gennaro, 2009), and were therefore themselves powerful symbols of the direct democracy and political spontaneity Grillo himself stood for. With the authority he had thus acquired, he was able in 2008 to begin to coordinate, and to establish principles for, a network of non-party lists by announcing the requisites and commitments that would apply to candidate lists wanting his certification and publicity through his blog. On the strength of the electoral results achieved by several of the lists in local elections in 2009, the M5S was launched in October of that year, taking 3.7% of the vote in the areas where it presented candidates at the 2010 regional elections, with a high of 7.0% in Emilia-Romagna.

As an entity the M5S was extremely difficult to categorize. On the one hand, it initially sought to encourage participatory and deliberative forms of democracy free of the control or mediation of the parties and institutions, and to make it possible for anyone wishing to do so to create a local group and thence field election candidates on behalf of the movement. On the other hand, it was only possible to use the movement's symbol with 'certification', given exclusively by Grillo as sole owner of the rights to use it, thus allowing him to exercise considerable power from the top down in sharp contrast to the principles of democracy. Its condemnation of established parties and institutions made it seem 'anti-political', yet such an image was belied by the explicit commitment of its activists to enhancing a politics of compromise and deliberation. Although M5S activists manifested a mistrust and rejection of conventional politics, a strong attachment to postmaterial issues such as the environment was suggestive of a very high level of commitment to the political process.

Its profile would become clearer with the passage of time. As it grew, it eventually became apparent that the M5S drew support from across the political spectrum as a function of its refusal to locate itself in leftright terms—this on the grounds that in a post-Cold War, post-ideological world, the terms no longer had meaning and that what counted, rather, were 'solutions'. Above all it offered itself as a vehicle of protest against the political establishment and the established parties with the promise, not just of a change of incumbents, but of an overhaul of the political system, to be based less on representative and more on direct forms of democracy. These features had a number of implications. As a 'catch-all' party, seeking support from wherever along the political spectrum it could find it, one of its 'taboos' (Bordignon and Ceccarini, 2019) concerned a rejection of alliances (as these would inevitably undermine such a strategy by forcing a left-right colouring upon it despite itself). Second, its claims were somewhat contradictory. On the one hand, its suggestion that politics was not about ideology but about resolving problems gave it a technocratic hue leading it to exalt those with special expertise. On the other hand, its anti-establishment profile led it to embrace the opposite assumptions, namely that ordinary people were just as well qualified to take on the positions of leadership normally reserved by the establishment for 'experts'. Third, its insistence that representatives were delegates, not trustees (as reflected, for example, in its opposition to Article 67 of the Constitution),[5] gave its appeal strongly populist overtones. That is, in claiming to be the only authentic representative of ordinary people in opposition to an oppressive elite, it ended up embracing the classic populist positions (1) that the only criterion that mattered from the point of view of democratic legitimacy was the backing of a majority and (2) that its opponents were illegitimate competitors for political office. Therefore, notwithstanding its early emphasis on participatory democracy, plebiscites and the counting of votes (which it practised frequently through online votes among its membership) were what counted for the purposes of democracy, not deliberation or minority rights.

On 21 December 2012 Monti resigned as Prime Minister, after the PdL announced, earlier in the month, that it would withdraw its support for the Government once the 2013 budget had been approved. Elections were due to be held by April 2013 in any case, but there appeared to be a number of advantages to the PdL in bringing the Government's term to an end earlier. One of these was that it would enable Berlusconi to seize the political initiative. For months after his resignation he had kept himself at the centre of media attention by first 'disappearing' from the scene and then making a series of assertions and counter-assertions about his intentions, thus fuelling constant speculation about his future. He now claimed that the Government's policies were proving unsuccessful and that this required him to make a comeback. One of the basic themes of his appeal, from the very start, had always been that as a successful businessman he had special talents not possessed by the average professional politician. Bringing the Government to an end might thereby block discussion of proposed changes to the electoral law that the PdL considered disadvantageous, as well as of proposals to limit eligibility for elected office of those with criminal convictions, which would be disadvantageous to Berlusconi. Furthermore, although the parties of the centre-right were far behind those of the centre-left in voting intention polls, about one-half of the electorate was undecided. Berlusconi therefore relied on the possibility of making a comeback, as he was widely credited with having done in 2006, by attempting to ride the populist tide of opinion now expressed by Grillo, and the growing disaffection with Monti and austerity. He was aware that with Grillo making inroads into the support bases of both the centre-left and the centre-right, he could actually secure the Camera dei Deputati (Chamber of Deputies) majority premium with a relatively small proportion of voters and electors—as, in fact, he almost succeeded in doing (Table 5.1).

In order to secure the regionally distributed majority premium in the Senato della Repubblica (Senate of the Republic), an alliance with the LN was indispensable for the PdL; so, although the two parties had adopted radically different stances towards the Monti Government, with the NL opposing it from the outset, the choices before voters at the February 2013 election included a centre-right coalition comprising these two parties and a few minor associations, only one of which

Table 5.1 General election results 2013, Chamber of Deputies

Parties/coalitions	Votes		Seats	
	Number	*%*	*Number*	*%*
PD	8,932,615	25.5	297	47.1
SEL	1,106,784	3.2	37	5.9
Others	328,216	0.9	11	1.7
Total Bersani coalition	10,367,615	29.6	345	54.8
PdL	7,478,796	21.3	98	15.6
LN	1,392,398	4.0	18	2.9
FdI	668,881	1.9	9	1.4
Others	534,034	1.5		
Total Berlusconi coalition	10,074,109	28.7	125	19.8
Movimento 5 Stelle	8,797,902	25.1	109	17.3
Civic Choice with Monti for Italy	3,004,739	8.6	39	6.2
UdC	609,565	1.7	8	1.3
FLI	159,332	0.5		
Total Monti coalition	3,773,636	10.8	47	7.5
Civil Revolution	781,098	2.2		
Others	1,262,927	3.6	4	0.6
Total	35,057,287		630	

Source: Based on data from D'Alimonte (2013, Table 1).

Note: The figures include the results for the Valle d'Aosta region and the foreign constituency.

achieved a share of the vote above 1%. On the centre-left, similar considerations were in favour of the PD, under its leader Pier Luigi Bersani, running in alliance, in the Italia. Bene Comune (Italy. Common Good) coalition, with Sinistra Ecologia Libertà (SEL—The Left, Ecology and Freedom), a left-wing grouping surrounding the president of the Puglia region, Nichi Vendola, who had broken with the Partito della Rifondazione Comunista (PRC—Communist Refoundation Party) in the aftermath of 2008. On the other hand, both could afford to exclude IdV, the PRC, the Partito dei Comunisti Italiani (Party of Italian Communists) and other small parties of the left, none of which had reached 2% in opinion polls. Unwanted by Italia. Bene Comune, the only chance they had of securing representation was as part of a joint list—Rivoluzione Civile (RC—Civil Revolution) under Public Prosecutor Antonio Ingroia—in which they would have to submerge their separate identities. This and the imperfect summability of their voters would, however, make it more difficult to surmount the 4% threshold—as in the end they failed to do.

Finally, the forces of the centre were brought together in Scelta Civica (SC—Civic Choice) under the leadership of Monti, who despite denials of any long-term political ambitions when he had become Prime Minister, now sought to continue in office, aware that the most widely expected election outcome was a coalition between Italia. Bene Comune and the centre. He made a mistake: the sacrifice of his *super partes* status, his inexperience as a politician and a poorly run campaign gave him too few seats in the Senate to make him decisive in government formation. In any case, as a life senator, he did not need to run for office. Had he remained *super partes* and retained the authority that went with it, then he might have been called upon to stay on as Prime Minister in the difficult political situation that followed the election.

The outcome appeared to mark the end of an era. Italia. Bene Comune won 29.6% of the vote in the election for the 630-seat Chamber of Deputies to take the 340-seat majority premium. The centre-right coalition won just 0.37% fewer votes than the centre-left, while the M5S took 25.6%. Thus, the country appeared to be divided into three essentially equal segments, with the only other two formations of any significance, SC and RC, taking 10.6% and 2.3%, respectively.

For Berlusconi, now almost 77 years of age, the outcome appeared to set the seal on his loss of office in 2011. His (narrow) failure to clinch office meant that from then on, although he would remain a party leader with a high profile on the Italian political stage, he would no longer set the agenda to the extent that he had done in the past. To an ever-increasing extent, his role would become confined to reacting to initiatives taken by others. And while in the run-up to the next general election, in 2018, it looked as though he might just emerge in the role of king-maker, that hope too was dashed, and by the end of the decade his party had been reduced to the small change of Italian politics.

The centre-left appeared, therefore, to have won in 2013, but this was only because, on a voter turnout that decreased from 80.5% in 2008 to 75.2% in 2013, its haemorrhaging of votes was somewhat less than that suffered by the centre-right. Furthermore, in the contest for the Senate, in which the majority premium was distributed region by region, the centre-left's 31.8% plurality left it 35 seats short of an overall majority. This would not have mattered had it not been for the fact that both the Chamber of Deputies and the Senate have co-equal legislative powers and governments must retain the confidence of both (a state of affairs known as 'symmetric bicameralism'), and that in the immediate aftermath of the election there did not appear to be a viable combination of parties capable of delivering that confidence. Thus, the election's outcome was a stalemate, one indicating that neither the consensual nor the majoritarian logics on which the formation of governments and the conduct of politics generally had hitherto rested could any longer be easily applied (Fabbrini and Lazar, 2013), and was in that sense too, a watershed. That is to say, the election outcome made it possible for the parties neither to reach some sort of post-election power-sharing arrangement that all could live with (as had been the approach to government formation until 1994), nor to govern on the basis of having been part of a group of parties that had won an overall majority of seats (which had been the approach from 1994 on).

In seeming to mark the end of one era, however, the outcome of the 2013 election also highlighted the considerable uncertainties of the new one. In the initial weeks following the election it became clear that, because it drew its support from across the left-right spectrum, the M5S would not sustain a centre-left, PD-led government in office; and because in the immediate aftermath there was no other combination of parties able and willing to come together to form a parliamentary majority either, it was not until 28 April, 62 days after polling, that a government could actually be formed and sworn in. Such delays are not unusual: for example, the first Government headed by Giuliano Amato, which held office from 28 June 1992 to 22 April 1993, was sworn in 83 days after the general election of 5 and 6 April 1992. However, the delay in 2013 was ended only because, as we shall see, the immediate aftermath of the election coincided with the need to elect a new President of the Republic, a circumstance that eventually forced the PD and the PdL to come together to form a government with SC and a small number of ministers without party affiliation.

Consequently, the Government that eventually came to power on 28 April 2013 under Enrico Letta, a 46-year-old former Christian Democrat and PD Deputy General Secretary, was a 'grand coalition'—the first in the history of the Republic—and included representatives of all three of the main alliances that had contested the February elections. Since the Government's two largest components—the PD and the PdL—had always had considerable difficulty in according each other legitimacy as potential governing actors, the Government had to be considered inherently fragile. At the same time, however, it was under considerable pressure to reform the institutions whose malfunctioning had been a significant contributor to the 2013 outcome in the first place, especially insofar as they had produced 'incompatible' election outcomes in the two branches of Parliament. The history of the legislature that was about to begin would be largely the history of efforts to get to grips with this problem, as we now go on to describe in the chapter that follows.

Notes

1 Article 138 of the Italian Constitution stipulates that amendments to it require each chamber of Parliament to vote in favour on two occasions separated by an interval of not less than three months; that those in favour must on the second occasion be a majority of the chambers' members (not just of those voting); and that citizens may subject the amendments to a referendum where, on the second occasion, they have been passed with the support of less than two-thirds of the members of one or both chambers.

2 These concerned legislation to circumvent a European Court judgment that television frequencies occupied by the Prime Minister's Retequattro should be ceded to a rival station, Europa 7, and proposals providing for the discretionary postponement of trials where charges did not involve issues of public safety—supposedly to help to increase the rate of throughput of the judicial system as a whole.

3 At the time of the Bicameral Commission for Constitutional Reform in 1997, for example, when it had sought the entrepreneur's cooperation by refraining from legislation to deal with his conflict of interests, the centre-left found that in the end, Berlusconi withdrew his cooperation anyway, leaving constitutional reform in tatters but his media empire intact.

4 According to a famous analogy made by the former socialist and legal scholar, Giuliano Amato, and cited by Pasquino (2003).

5 This stipulates that members of Parliament carry out their duties without a binding mandate. Moreover, in office from 2018, the M5S secured legislation which would reduce the number of deputies from 630 to 400, and the number of senators from 315 to 200.

6   A bridge between two worlds
The 17th legislature

In the initial weeks following the election it became clear that the
MoVimento 5 Stelle (M5S—Five Star Movement) faced a dilemma: if
it allowed a PD-led government to take office, then some of its supporters would accuse it of 'selling out'; however, if it refused to do so,
then it risked losing its more moderate supporters. Pier Luigi Bersani's
hope, then, was that he could persuade a sufficient number of M5S
senators to allow him to become Prime Minister, knowing that any
agreement with Silvio Berlusconi would be unacceptable to a majority,
if not all, of his party members. Berlusconi and the Popolo della Libertà (PdL—People of Freedom) called for a broad coalition involving
them and the Partito Democratico (PD—Democratic Party) in the
national interest—aware, in all likelihood, that such a scenario would
assist Berlusconi personally. Among other things, in November 2012
Berlusconi had appealed against a conviction for tax fraud and a five-
year ban on holding public office, and it seemed likely that before too
long the Senato della Repubblica (Senate of the Republic) would have
to decide whether or not to expel him from the Parlamento (Parliament). He probably calculated that if the appeal were to go against
him, then this would put PD parliamentarians under pressure to help
him by, for example, refraining from voting to lift his parliamentary
immunity—this as the price of the Government's survival.

On 22 March 2013 President Napolitano gave Bersani what is
known as a *preincarico* (conditional mandate) for the formation of a
government. The move reflected the formal procedure whereby governments are appointed and take office in Italy. Thus, new governments
receive, from outgoing governments, all of the relevant powers and
responsibilities the moment they are sworn in by the President of the
Republic—but *before* obtaining the confidence of Parliament, which
they must do within 10 days of the swearing-in ceremony. Therefore,
presidents only give full mandates if they believe, having consulted the

political parties, that the person so chosen is likely to be successful in getting the forces in Parliament to agree on a government and programme capable of commanding a majority; only then do they proceed to the swearing in of the ministers proposed by the Prime Minister-designate. Thus, the President was in effect telling Bersani that his task was to assist the President's consultations by carrying out one or more rounds of consultations of his own and then reporting on the outcome, which, if positive, would have led to his being given a full mandate to form a government.

Bersani's fundamental problem was that his coalition was 36 seats short of a majority in the Senate. Scelta Civica's (Civic Choice) 21 seats were insufficient to make up the difference; the M5S had 54. If he could persuade a sufficient number of the senators belonging to parties or coalitions other than his own to absent themselves at the moment of the confirmatory confidence vote, then in theory he could become Prime Minister at the head of a minority government whose measures Beppe Grillo had indicated his party would be willing to support on a case by case basis. There were two fundamental obstacles in the way of such a 'solution': first, Napolitano would not in any event—and even less so in view of the economic crisis—confer a full mandate on Bersani in the absence of assurances about the likelihood of his being able to assemble a parliamentary majority that would be stable; second, providing such assurances could not dispense with prior agreement among the forces that would support the incoming government on what its programme would be. The vote of confidence which a new government asks for is a vote either for or against the Prime Minister, the composition of the government *and* the programme on the basis of which the government seeks Parliament's support. This meant that a minority government was not an option and the PD leader ultimately had no alternative—if he were to look to M5S support for a centre-left-led government—to trying to persuade M5S senators to join him in coalition on the basis of a package of policy proposals that had been agreed in advance.

The story of Bersani's efforts to mobilize his own followers behind such a strategy, and to break down resistance to it within the ranks of the M5S, is one I have described elsewhere (Newell, 2014, 2016). In the final analysis, his efforts foundered on the intransigence of Grillo who in turn was in a position to force the M5S's newly elected parliamentarians to fall into line behind him. His ownership of the Movement's symbol, which we mentioned in the previous chapter, in effect gave him the power to expel dissidents and effectively end their political careers. Second, his exceptionally high media profile, gave him the power to punish dissidents in an especially public manner. Third, the 'Code of Conduct for representatives of the Five Star Movement elected to Parliament', which had appeared on the M5S website shortly after the election, reinforced Grillo's power by stipulating, among other things, that voting in the chambers was to conform to the decisions taken by a majority of the group's members, and that parliamentary voting decisions were to be explained and justified daily by means of a video published on the Movement's YouTube channel. Grillo's intransigence, in turn, stemmed from his awareness that he had to oppose an alliance with the PD as the cost of keeping united a following without a precise identity other than opposition to the established parties, one without roots in a specific social stratum or strong organization on the ground.

Consequently, when on 28 March 2013 Bersani went to the presidential palace, he was obliged to report that his consultations had not resulted in a solution to the problem of the formation of a government—which was only resolved thanks to the fact that President Napolitano was close to the end of his seven-year term, and to the opportunity this gave him—through the politics underlying the voting that now took place for his successor—to force a resolution to the crisis.

On 18 April 2013 Parliament and representatives of the regions assembled to elect a presidential successor to Napolitano, in accordance with Article 83 of the Constitution. A two-thirds' majority (672 votes) was required in the first three ballots, and a simple majority (508) from the fourth. The PD and Sinistra, Ecologia, Libertà (SEL— The Left, Ecology and Freedom) commanded 496 votes. The agreed Berlusconi-Bersani candidate was a Catholic former trade unionist, Franco Marini. He, however, suffered from defections on the part of SEL and PD left-wingers, who preferred the M5S's choice of a left-wing candidate, Stefano Rodotà. On 19 April the fourth ballot failed to produce a result and Romano Prodi was fielded as the centre-left candidate. However, Prodi, who was opposed by Berlusconi, was damaged by those within the PD who believed that resolution of the crisis surrounding the formation of a government required reaching an understanding with Berlusconi. Bersani then seems to have concluded that only Napolitano (with a background as a prominent leader of the former PCI and by then an elder statesperson) could guarantee the PD vote. Berlusconi willingly supported the idea of a re-edition of the Napolitano presidency, as he was known to want the 'reliable' government that Berlusconi himself advocated, and Napolitano made it clear that the formation of such a government was the condition to his agreeing, at the age of 88, to the unprecedented move of seeking a second term. Napolitano was thus re-elected on 20 April with 738 votes in his favour, SEL and the M5S once again voting for Rodotà. On 28 April 2013 Enrico Letta was sworn in as Prime Minister. His close working relationship with his uncle, Gianni Letta, one of Berlusconi's most trusted advisers, was regarded as an important means of building connection and trust between the two largest, centre-left and centre-right, coalitions.

The relationship seemed crucial, for there were few informed observers who expected the Government to survive in office for very long. The PD (for many of whose members it was an article of faith that Berlusconi's conflict of interests made him inherently illegitimate as a contender for office) had agreed to the coalition under duress. Berlusconi—now ahead in the polls, in a situation of economic crisis and with no alternative government seemingly possible—wielded enormous blackmail power he could use to pursue *ad personam* legislation which would be destabilizing either because it would be difficult for his coalition partners to accept or because it would allow him to bring the Government down on a suitable pretext. Finally, the two main partners were sharply divided on issues of high salience for voters such as the Imposta Municipale Unica (Single Council Tax). As we shall now explain, Berlusconi did indeed attempt to undermine the Government and it did not last for very long—but it was not Berlusconi who was responsible for its demise.

Exploited by the PdL as a means of maintaining its distinctive profile within the coalition, the issue of taxation was the source of frequent conflict between the governing partners in early and mid-2013 and gave rise to periodic PdL threats to walk out of the coalition. Matters came to a head in September. The programmatic statement that Letta had made when asking for the confirmatory votes of confidence at the end of April had referred to a commitment to abandoning a planned rise in value-added tax (VAT) which had been provided for by the Monti Government and was due to come into effect on 1 October. A decree law[1] was required to bring about a postponement of the rise until 1 January while it was planned to use the 2014 Finance Law to resolve the matter definitively. Meanwhile, in late September PdL parliamentarians threatened to resign en masse out of solidarity with Berlusconi whose future was to be the subject of a vote by the Senate electoral committee on 4 October. On that date the committee would decide whether, in accordance with the Severino law[2] passed by the Monti Government, to recommend to the Senate that it vote in favour of Berlusconi's expulsion after the Court of Appeal had upheld his conviction for tax fraud in May and after the Court of Cassation had done so on 1 August, meaning that the conviction was now definitive. As a consequence, on 27 September the Cabinet decided to postpone discussion of deferring the planned VAT rise on the grounds that the PdL parliamentarians' threat created such uncertainty about the Government's capacity to pursue its programme that there needed to be prior clarification, through a confidence vote in Parliament, about whether it could carry on. Thus, when it was announced on 28 September that PdL ministers would resign, the reason given—the failure of the Cabinet to guarantee that the VAT rise would not go ahead on 1 October—was widely judged to be a pretext.

Berlusconi presumably calculated that if he succeeded in bringing the Government down, he could provoke fresh elections, which might enable him to avoid the consequences of 1 August. Although the outcome of a new poll could not be taken for granted, voting intention data were not discouraging either and the PD might suffer most from any government collapse if Berlusconi could frame the event as an attempt to thwart moves by the centre-left to raise taxes as part of the following year's budget proposals. The risk was that collapse might provoke turmoil in the financial markets, for which the PdL could be blamed.

It was presumably the awareness of this risk that led each of the ministers 'ordered' by Berlusconi to resign to line up one by one to express their misgivings until it became apparent that the threat to bring the Government down might provoke a major party split. From this it became clear that, Berlusconi's stance notwithstanding, the Government would survive the confidence vote, scheduled for 2 October 2013, anyway. Hence the sense of high drama associated with it when, during the preceding debate, the entrepreneur entered the Senate chamber suddenly to announce a humiliating climb-down: he and his followers would support the Government in the no confidence motion. This was a dramatic new development in Italian politics as well as a dramatic last-minute U-turn: for the first time, Berlusconi, the leader of a 'personal party' created by him and for him, had been forced to bow to the will of his followers. The assumption that the Government was weak because it depended on the cooperation of Berlusconi who had the power to withdraw the support of his followers any time he wished had been put to the test and found wanting.

Matters then got worse for the entrepreneur. When, in November 2013, the Senate accepted the recommendation of its electoral committee that Berlusconi should be deprived of his parliamentary seat, he was unable to persuade sufficient numbers of his followers to ensure that the vote on the recommendation went in his favour by again threatening the Government's survival. Several of his followers now left to form their own party, the Nuovo Centrodestra (NCD—New Centre Right), and in so doing again confirmed that thanks to his advanced age, Berlusconi no longer enjoyed the unassailable authority over the centre-right that he once had. With the NCD continuing in government, he and the remainder of the PdL went into opposition as a relaunched Forza Italia (FI—Forward Italy, or Come on Italy!). However, if this suggested that the Government was more stable than it had seemed at the outset, then contemporaneous developments within the PD soon revealed that appearances were deceptive, for just 13 weeks later Letta was forced to resign to make way for the formation of a new Government led by fellow PD spokesperson, Matteo Renzi.

On 8 December 2013 Renzi had scored a resounding victory in the 'primary' election for the leadership of the PD—an election that had been made necessary by the resignation of Bersani in the wake of the PD's disappointing performance in the February general election and his failure to form a government thereafter. Renzi won the leadership election due mainly to his status as the 'change candidate', who had earned the nickname *il Rottamatore* (the scrapper) thanks to his insistence that the PD, to win a general election, needed to undergo fundamental renewal based on a generational turnover among its leaders and principal spokespeople. Renzi owed his success to a number of factors: his communication skills, which were often compared to those of Berlusconi and which had a significant effect on television and among ordinary people; his non-ideological, 'catch-all' brand of politics, which appeared to offer the prospect of enabling his party to appeal to voters outside of its traditional base, which led to comparisons with former British Prime Minister, Tony Blair. Furthermore, he offered a less jarring version of the virulent 'anti-political' condemnation of established parties and institutions that was the hallmark of Grillo and the M5S. For all these reasons, Renzi, who at the time of the leadership contest was the charismatic incumbent mayor of Florence, was viewed as the candidate best placed to increase the capacity of party and political system to resist the growth of the M5S and the anti-political sentiments underlying it, and to respond to parties' growing requirements for politicians able to act as celebrities, exploiting the growing opportunities for individual actors to affect politics through the mobilization of public opinion.

Renzi had never hidden his ambitions to become Prime Minister, and in early February 2014 he managed to persuade his party's Direzione Nazionale—the executive committee of the PD's supreme policymaking body, the Assemblea Nazionale—to pass a motion speaking of 'the urgent need to initiate a new phase with a different executive'. Although the motion made no mention of Renzi taking Letta's place, this, given the context in which it was passed, was understood by all concerned to be its political significance; and given the dependence of the party's deputies' political careers on the executive committee and the general secretary, they could be expected to fall into line. Letta understood that he had been deserted and resigned as premier on 22 February. As expected, President Napolitano duly conferred a mandate on Renzi who thus became leader of the 65th Italian Government since the end of the Second World War.

The sense that Italy might be standing on the threshold of a new, happier era, was reinforced by three developments in the months after Renzi ascended to the premiership. First, his new Government displayed significant features of novelty. At the age of 39, Renzi was the youngest Prime Minister in Italian history; with the average age of the Cabinet just 47, the Government was the youngest in the history of the Republic. With only 16 ministers, eight of whom were women, the Government also stood out for its small size and its gender balance. These features seemed to augur well for the realization of popular hopes of a new era in Italian politics, for they were in keeping with the promises of fundamental renewal based on a displacement of traditional oligarchies that had been the hallmark of Renzi's appeal during the course of his rise to power.

Second, the agreement Renzi had reached with Berlusconi in January 2014 on a new electoral law seemed initially to give Italy the best prospects for much-needed reform that it had had for the past decade. As we have seen, reform was made urgent by the fact that the electoral law of 2005—which, despite symmetric bicameralism, provided for different systems for the two chambers of Parliament—had twice brought the country to the brink of ungovernability—once after the election of 2006 and again after the election of February 2013—thus contributing to the growth of popular disenchantment that had fuelled the explosion of support for the M5S at the general election of 2013. The prospects for reform seemed much better than they had been hitherto because, despite internal disquiet, the two largest parties promoting it together commanded a clear majority in Parliament, and both had a strong incentive to achieve success.

That incentive derived from the M5S which in 2013 had taken votes from both the centre-left and the centre-right. Thus, on 12 March 2014 the Camera dei Deputati (Chamber of Deputies) approved proposals for electoral law reform, which envisaged a closed-list system of proportional representation, with exclusion thresholds, a run-off ballot and a majority premium for the winning list or coalition of lists. The calculation was that, as the M5S had a support base and political project that rendered it 'non-coalitionable', it would find it almost impossible to make it through to any run-off ballot. The proposals were amended during the course of the following 13 months, and as finally enacted on 4 May 2015, the reform (referred to, in shorthand, as the 'Italicum') provided that only single lists, not coalitions of lists, would be allowed to run. Thanks to its provision for a majority premium to be awarded to the most-voted list as opposed to the single most-voted coalition, it aimed to improve the cohesiveness of the winning majority by preventing it from achieving power through the construction of the large unwieldy coalitions (such as those that had been the distinctive feature of the 2006 elections) which were designed to win elections but which were incapable of governing. Any list achieving at least 40% of the vote nationally would automatically receive 340 of the 630 seats in the Chamber of Deputies; 278 seats would be shared among the remaining eligible lists, and 12 seats were assigned to the overseas constituency for Italians resident abroad.[3] In the event of no list obtaining 40% of the vote, there would be a run-off ballot between the two lists obtaining the most votes, with the majority premium going to the winner. The legislation came into force on 1 July 2016.

The third development giving cause for optimism was the outcome of the elections to the European Parliament held on 25 May 2014. As elsewhere in the European Union (EU), in Italy the electoral campaign focused less on the Strasbourg and Brussels assemblies—or what their members did at the European level—than on national issues and the distribution of support between domestic politicians, policy positions and parties in the national arena. Renzi knew that if the PD did well in the European elections, such an outcome would strengthen his hold over his party and, therefore, his ability to pursue reforms that were provoking significant internal divisions. In the event, the PD emerged as by far and away the largest party, almost double the size of the second-placed M5S which, with 21% of the vote, had lost support compared with its share of 25.6% in the general election of February 2013. It was an outcome that was widely interpreted as an indication of the capacity of *il Rottamatore* to cut the ground from under the feet of the M5S with promises of political renewal.

Renzi's authority seemed to be further reinforced by the circumstances surrounding the election of a new President of the Republic in January 2015. On 14 January, shortly after the end of Italy's tenure of the rotating presidency of the EU, the 89-year-old President

Napolitano resigned, making way for the election of a new incumbent. The election of a new president was significant for two reasons. First, although presidents are obliged to be and to be seen to be at all times *super partes*, the identity of the person chosen for the role matters to parties. This is because, although *super partes*, presidents can never be 'neutral' in the sense that they *never* take decisions driven by consideration of their substantive political consequences. Second, therefore, the outcome of presidential elections affects the authority of parties and their leaders. This latter consideration was of more than usual relevance in the case of the 2015 election since the previous January Renzi and Berlusconi had reached an agreement known as the Patto del Nazareno (Nazarene Pact) making provision for wide-ranging constitutional reform to complement the reform of the electoral law discussed above. Renzi was therefore aware that the solidity of the pact depended on being able to find a presidential candidate who was congenial to the entrepreneur. He was also aware, however, that the PD was internally divided over the reform proposals and the collaboration with Berlusconi that they entailed, and that therefore it could not be relied upon to vote for a candidate acceptable to Berlusconi. Given this dilemma, what transpired in the presidential election was that both Renzi and Berlusconi invited their followers to cast blank ballots at the first three rounds of voting, which required two-thirds' majorities, aiming to postpone the real negotiations to the fourth round when a simple majority was all that was required. However, just before the fourth round on 31 January, Renzi announced his endorsement of the candidature of Sergio Mattarella—a Constitutional Court judge who had once resigned as Minister of Education in 1990 in protest at legislation that enabled Berlusconi to expand his media empire—without Berlusconi's agreement.

As a widely respected politician who had been prominent in the fight against the Mafia, Mattarella would not only attract relatively cohesive support on the centre-left but would attract the support of many on the centre-right too. Berlusconi was thus left with a choice: either support Mattarella and appear to have caved in to Renzi, or urge his supporters to continue to cast blank ballots in the fourth round of voting, knowing that in the secrecy of the polling booth some might disobey him—with a corresponding dent to his authority. Ultimately, he chose the latter option and the blow to his authority was duly delivered: Mattarella was elected with 665 votes, almost a two-thirds' majority, in the process revealing a major split in Berlusconi's party, since the number of blank ballots was about 40 less than the number of his followers (Newell and Giovannini, 2015).

Mattarella's election was of profound significance for the remainder of Renzi's term of office as Prime Minister. It represented the high point of the Florentine's power and authority. On the one hand, up until then he had been vulnerable to criticism within and outside his party (especially from the M5S) that the Nazarene Pact was a kind of unholy alliance, probably based on an exchange of favours, not all of which were likely to be legitimate. What the outcome of the presidential election did, then, was considerably to enhance his authority by suggesting that he was far less beholden to Berlusconi and his interests than his critics had hitherto argued. On the other hand, since some among Berlusconi's followers felt that they had been out-manoeuvred by Renzi by having his candidate imposed upon them, it undermined the Nazarene Pact and the reform process, ultimately bringing about the Prime Minister's decline and fall, as we shall now explain.

In the immediate term, he was shielded from danger by the fact that the Italicum had already been approved by the Senate, with FI support, on 27 January 2015. To reach the statute book, it had now to be passed only by the lower house—where Renzi knew he would have the parliamentary numbers to get his way with or without FI, because he could deal with the dissident minority in his own party by making the issue a matter of confidence in his Government. In the end, therefore, the reform was passed into law, with every major political player able to emerge from the process with their political authority more or less intact: when it came to the final vote, the parties opposed to the Government, including FI, were able to desert the Chamber of Deputies in protest against the dubious legitimacy of using the question of confidence to secure the kind of legislation that ought only to be passed with broad cross-party agreement. This enabled Renzi's internal critics to make a stand by voting against the measure in the knowledge that it would not bring the Government down, and this in turn allowed Renzi to secure the reform on which he had staked his reputation.

However, a new electoral law was only one aspect of the institutional overhaul that seemed necessary and that Renzi was seeking to achieve. Given that the new law applied to the Chamber of Deputies only, and given symmetric bicameralism, governability required either an identical electoral law for the Senate or a change in the institution's constitutional status. The path chosen, and the one written into the Nazarene Pact, had been the latter, since symmetric bicameralism, by making it necessary for proposed legislation to shuttle between the two chambers of Parliament until such time as identically agreed texts could be agreed by both, was widely perceived as a major source of governing inefficiency.[4]

It was always clear that the reform of the Senate—which involved limiting its size, its legislative powers and its powers to install and unseat governments—would be difficult to achieve as it would require constitutional changes. These, in accordance with Article 138 of the Constitution, can be made only on the basis of not one, but two, separate votes in favour of identically worded texts in each of the chambers with a delay of not less than three months between the votes; furthermore, the votes can be made the subject of a popular referendum if passed with less than a two-thirds' majority on the second vote of either of the two chambers. The difficulties—in a context of weak and divided parties and questions concerning the reform paradox, i.e. the extent to which senators could be expected reliably to support change that would involve them in voting themselves out of office—were not long in making themselves felt. Therefore, it was not until 12 April 2016 that the proposed reform's parliamentary passage was completed, and it had been clear to all concerned that the parliamentary arithmetic would make it impossible for the reform's supporters to avoid having to clear the additional hurdle of the confirmatory popular referendum. Consequently, as soon as 12 April had come and gone, parliamentarians of both the governing majority and the opposition rushed to the Court of Cassation to deposit the necessary signatures for a referendum. In September the Government announced that the plebiscite would be held on 4 December.

In the referendum, voters were asked to accept or reject, alongside the proposed reform of the Senate, various additional constitutional changes of varying significance. Their common denominator was an attempt significantly to reduce the number of veto points throughout the political system, and thereby to enhance policymakers' capacity for decisive decision-making. Thus, besides depriving the Senate of parity with the Chamber of Deputies, the package of reforms envisaged, among other things, a redefinition of the powers of the regions in the interests of reducing the considerable volume of time-wasting litigation before the Constitutional Court that had arisen from the concurrent powers enjoyed by the state and the regions since 2001 (when in the dying days of the 13th legislature, the centre-left had secured reform of Title V of the Constitution increasing the powers of the regions and hoping, thereby, to take the wind out of the sails of the Lega Nord (LN—Northern League).

Lined up on the 'Yes' side were the PD and its governing allies, most notably the NCD and the forces of the centre. The 'No' side brought together the parties of opposition, which principally comprised FI, the LN and the M5S, and which were aware of the reforms' close association with the Prime Minister (who had made it clear from the day he took office that they were the principal criterion by which he wanted his term of office to be judged). The parties were therefore aware that to support the proposals was to enhance the fortunes of Renzi, and that, in a world of mediatized and personalized politics, to enhance the fortunes of Renzi was to prolong their own exclusion from power. In the referendum campaign Renzi was also opposed, more or less explicitly, by an assortment of critics within his own party and by forces further to the left.

The outcome was a 59% to 41% defeat for Renzi's reforms—a defeat that had been gathering momentum as the campaign progressed. Initially, opinion polls had suggested a clear referendum victory for the Prime Minister, but Renzi's lead narrowed considerably after 12 April 2016 when the two sides in the campaign began to square up to each other, while the 'No' side gained an increasing advantage as Renzi's fortunes declined on other fronts.

In the first place, while he had presented himself as an 'anti-establishment' figure in an attempt to beat the M5S at its own game, his simultaneous attempt to construct a 'personalized', leader-dominated party had been opposed by internal critics who were more wedded to traditional, mass party conceptions of what the PD should be. Second, the autocratic way in which he had forced through reform in a number of other areas, notably in the labour market and education, had alienated powerful interest groups. In December 2014 the so-called Jobs Act had authorized the Government to pass, over a period of months, a series of legislative decrees with significant implications for workers' terms and conditions of employment. Meanwhile, employment protection legislation, already watered down by the Monti administration during 2011–13, was further restricted. Applauded by the European Commission and the International Monetary Fund (IMF), the measures were criticized by trade unions and many on the left, and met with public protests.

In 2015 the so-called Buona Scuola (Good School) reform was greeted in a similar fashion. While the Buona Scuola reforms sought to respond to criticisms from the Bank of Italy and international bodies that the schools system was a major contributor to Italy's economic weakness, opponents argued that one of the major consequences of the measures was likely to be a growing division between high-performing schools in affluent areas and substandard schools in poorer ones, with a consequent 'postcode lottery' of the kind that existed in the United Kingdom.

In 2016 Renzi had been quick to claim that encouraging increases in the rate of employment—which rose by a cumulative 1.1% in the period from March to June—were the consequence of the aforementioned reforms; but whatever the truth, the latter were ineffective in halting the decline in his popularity, as was a third significant reform achieved by his Government: the introduction of legislation permitting same-sex civil partnerships, which came into force on 5 June 2016.

Thus, local council elections held in the same month were apparently used by voters as an opportunity to reward or punish national-level politicians, with victories for the M5S in important cities such as Turin and Rome being widely interpreted both as a significant defeat for Renzi and as confirmation that he had by then become caught up in the same vicious circle that had engulfed prime ministers before him, whereby declining authority and capacity to govern produced declining popularity and diminishing authority in a vicious downward spiral. The constitutional referendum having come to be framed as a plebiscite on himself and his performance as Prime Minister, this is what the vote became in reality, and he duly resigned on 5 December.

Renzi, in the aftermath of the referendum, was widely thought to have been the architect of his own downfall insofar as he chose to accept the assumption that the referendum was a vote on him personally and indeed chose positively to encourage such framing. More plausible is that he had little choice in the matter. Given that this was the spin that was being put on the vote in the media and by all of his opponents, to attempt to deny it, to suggest that the outcome would have no bearing on his incumbency would have made him look weak and determined to cling onto power at all costs. It would have been to say, in effect, that he did not actually believe in the constitutional reforms he was seeking to promote. The only credible response was to accept the challenge that was being thrown down and to attempt to rise to it.

Three things seem to have been responsible for Renzi's fall. First, in seeking to build his political fortunes on the claim to be a political outsider who would take the establishment by storm, he was in essence seeking to deploy the same sort of strategy that Berlusconi had deployed before him, indeed to be a Berlusconi of the left. And just as Berlusconi had raised expectations and gone into decline when it became apparent that the promised 'new Italian miracle' was beyond his power to deliver, so it was that Renzi's career had followed a similar trajectory—albeit that the rise and fall took place over a shorter time span. Second, he was an ideologically agnostic politician willing to build in Parliament whatever alliances were necessary to achieve the objectives he had set himself. In essence, therefore, his political strategy had two strands to it. On the one hand, believing that the traditional principles of the left were outdated and stood in the way of the most urgently needed reforms, he sought to build support, like Berlusconi, through novel ways of communicating but without paying much attention to the underlying substance of messages. On the other hand, he sought to mobilize and sustain support by adopting a strictly pragmatic approach to the resolution of disputes, and including whatever parties were necessary in constructing the majorities needed to drive through reforms as quickly as possible.

This fed into the third factor, the management of his party. By the time he became Prime Minister, the PD had become a party among whose supporters anti-political sentiments had become widespread (Vignati, 2013). It was also a party whose statute—by undermining, as we mentioned in the previous chapter, the organizations of the 'party on the ground'—disincentivized membership driven by ideals, while incentivizing members who for more or less opportunistic reasons could be persuaded to fall in behind a leader, like Renzi, whose personal qualities appeared to, and for a time did, hold out the prospect of restoring the party's fortunes. If all of this assisted Renzi's rise and made it possible for him to dominate his party once he had become leader (to the extent that it gave rise to satirical media references to the 'PDR', the 'Partito di Renzi', or 'the Renzi Party'), then it also meant that when he attempted to pursue reforms with other parties whose platforms were different from those of the PD, he inevitably provoked internal opposition mobilized by other leaders and spokespeople. A good example of this sort of thing was the Jobs Act which, in seeking to abolish some of the clauses of Article 18 of the Workers' Statute, providing protection against unfair dismissal, attacked a piece of legislation considered by those on the left in Italy to represent one of their greatest post-war achievements.

Thus, he was unable to line up his party unitedly behind his constitutional reform proposals, that were seen by many in his party as representing an attempt to achieve in the wider political system the unhealthily autocratic management of power he was pursuing within his own party. The Italicum, for instance, made it possible, if not likely, that a list could win an absolute seat majority—in a Chamber of Deputies relatively free of constraints from the Senate—even if it had no more than a relatively small minority of votes. By virtue of the influence it gave party leaders (through their control over the composition of the party lists) to determine who was elected, it also arguably undermined the capacity of their parliamentary followers to hold party leaders to account.

The Government which replaced Renzi's, under the outgoing Prime Minister's foreign secretary, Paolo Gentiloni, was understood by all concerned from the outset to be an interim, caretaker, government, whose task was to preside over the affairs of the nation until early 2018 when the legislature would reach the end of its natural term. One of the most important tasks it would have to face would be reform of the electoral law, for now that Renzi had lost his referendum, the country was in the unsustainable position of having two very different laws for the Chamber of Deputies and the Senate, with the possibility, if not the likelihood, that any election fought on the basis of them would throw up two radically contrasting majorities in the two branches despite their having identical legislative powers.

The Government would also have to contend with the ever-increasing dimensions of the ongoing refugee crisis. Thanks to several drivers such as conflict in Syria and Libya, climate change and global social networks, since 2013 the crisis had seen thousands of refugees trying to reach Italy by boat from across the Mediterranean and thousands dying in the process. By the end of May 2017 more than 50,000 migrants had arrived in Italy by sea since the beginning of the year, an increase of 47% over the corresponding period for the previous year. The Government responded by continuing the efforts of the Renzi administration to persuade fellow EU member states to take a more active role in managing the crisis, perceiving, not without some justification, that Italy was not receiving the support it might be entitled to expect from its European partners. In February 2017 it reached an agreement with the fragile Government of Libya, committing the latter to taking more strenuous measures to reduce the flows of migrants from North Africa. In April, it secured legislation to streamline the procedures for processing applications for asylum. By these means it hoped to reduce the space available to the parties of the right to make political capital out of the crisis; however, although its measures were successful in reducing the number of arrivals (there were a total of 119,369 sea arrivals in 2017 and 23,370 in 2018, followed by a further decline, to 11,471, the following year,[5] they failed to prevent immigration dominating the 2018 election campaign or to prevent the anti-immigrant League from making a striking advance.

In June 2017 the Government committed funds of up to €17,000m. in an effort to stave off the threat of a run on two banks, Veneto Banca and Banca Popolare di Vicenza, both important lenders in Italy's north-eastern industrial heartland. The European Commission approved the rescue package, even though it appeared to breach EU rules requiring banks' creditors, especially bondholders, to take losses prior to the intervention of the public sector. While bondholders are normally professionals able to take such losses, Italy is an unusual case. According to the IMF, about one-third of Italian bank bonds are held by retail investors, and the prospect of retail losses added a considerable element of political risk not only within Italy but with repercussions for the EU, since an insistence that small retail investors take losses seemed likely to stoke support for the Eurosceptic M5S.

Also in June 2017, a new economic forecast from the Organisation for Economic Co-operation and Development (OECD) projected that Italy's gross domestic product would grow by 1.0% in 2017 and by 0.8% in 2018. The report suggested that business investment was strengthening, but that the stock of non-performing loans (NPLs) and the low profitability of the banking sector was limiting credit, especially to small and medium-sized enterprises, which account for a comparatively large proportion of the Italian economy. Thus, while it appeared that the economy was showing some fragile signs of improvement, there seemed little likelihood of any dramatic recovery in the more or less immediate future. Ultimately, growth for 2017 came in at 1.7% and if this was not much to cheer about, it did mean that there had been an improvement in the rate every year since the start of the legislature when it had stood at an alarming –1.8%.[6]

Consequently, by the end of the legislature, the Gentiloni Government had, if not an outstanding, at least a creditable record to defend. Signs of improvement had strengthened, with the economy—as one heavily dependent on exports—benefiting from the broader upswing in Europe. The stock of NPLs had begun to fall, as had unemployment, with the Government receiving praise from the OECD and in other quarters for a series of structural reforms, implemented or initiated in previous years, deemed essential to raising productivity and investment. All of this might have seemed to augur well for the PD as the mainstay of the government at the general election called for 4 March 2018, but voting intention polls suggested otherwise. By the end of December 2017, the PD was running at around 22%, down by 5% from its position six months earlier, while the opposition centre-right parties and the M5S had made gains of varying magnitude. Local elections in June, and the Sicilian regional elections on 5 November, had marked a revival in the political fortunes of FI and Silvio Berlusconi. The steady growth in popularity of the M5S was especially noteworthy as it came despite periodic accusations of poor judgement on the part of some of its representatives (notably the mayor of Rome, Virginia Raggi) and occasional allegations of improbity on the part of others. At the end of 2017, then, Italy faced an imminent general election whose outcome seemed impossible to predict. What did in fact happen before, during and after the general election is the matter to which we turn our attention in the chapter that follows.

Notes

1 Decree laws are laws which governments can introduce on their own authority but which Parliament must convert into ordinary legislation within 60 days if they are retain their validity beyond that time.

2 This bans those convicted of crimes carrying a penalty of two years or more from being members of Parliament or holding other public offices and renders them ineligible to stand as candidates for such offices for at least six years. In deference to the separation-of-powers principle and in accordance with article 66 of the Constitution which reserves to Parliament the power to determine the eligibility of its members, the Senate itself would have to decide whether Severino applied in Berlusconi's case.

3 As the result of a constitutional amendment sponsored in 2000 by AN parliamentarian, Mirko Tremaglia, a special constituency was created for Italians resident abroad. They had hitherto had to travel back to the Italian municipality in which they had last been resident if they were to exercise their right to vote. The expectation was that by making it easier for expatriates to vote the reform would favour the right. Since the reform was first implemented for the 2006 election, if anything, the reverse has been the case.

4 Inaccurately, as it so happens. The Italian legislature is in all probability more productive than it would be if it were mono-cameral since symmetric bicameralism makes it is possible to introduce and to process two legislative proposals simultaneously. As Pasquino and Pelizzo (2016) point out, though much criticised, symmetric bicameralism enables the Italian parliament to produce more laws, more quickly, than its counterparts in France, Germany, the UK and the United States.

5 United Nations High Commissioner for Refugees data available at https://data2.unhcr.org/en/situations/mediterranean/location/5205.

6 World Bank data available at https://data.worldbank.org/indicator/NY.GDP.MKTP.KD.ZG?locations=IT&view=chart.

7 The 2018 general election and its aftermath

Italia quo vadis?

On 25 January 2017, six weeks after the Gentiloni Government had taken office, the Constitutional Court (or the Consulta[1] as it is colloquially referred to) declared unconstitutional certain parts of the 'Italicum', in a case that arose from attempts by opponents of the law to challenge it in the courts. The case was eloquent about the role of the Constitutional Court in Italian politics.

Beginning in February 2016 a number of civil society groups, constitutional lawyers and internal opponents of Matteo Renzi had come together in the Coordinamento per la Democrazia Costituzionale (Coordinating Group for Constitutional Democracy) to challenge the Italicum on several grounds.[2] Italian constitutional law differs from its equivalent in other jurisdictions such as the German and the Spanish in denying to individuals the right of direct access to judgments of constitutional legitimacy on the grounds that their constitutional rights have been violated. Instead, such controversies come before the ordinary courts, wherein the outcome requires a judgment of constitutional legitimacy in order to enable the judge in question to decide the case. Consequently, the various individuals and groups interested in challenging the electoral law were obliged to bring cases against the Prime Minister's Office and the Ministry of the Interior before the ordinary courts, asking them to recognize that their constitutionally guaranteed democratic rights had been damaged by the Italicum whose legitimacy therefore required testing before the Constitutional Court. In order to act, a court must be persuaded that the appellant has a genuine interest at stake in the decision it is asked to make; and here, since no election under the Italicum had actually taken place, success in persuading the courts to refer the matter relied on the argument that voting was a 'permanent' and 'inviolable' right whose exercise could take place at any time. Hence, any uncertainty surrounding it did give rise to a genuine interest that could only be protected by removal of the uncertainty and therefore by a Constitutional Court decision (Newell, 2017).

To many observers, this looked suspiciously like giving direct access to the Court by the back door and in any case represented a further twist in the process of what has come to be known as the 'judicialization of politics'. This is a growing tendency, in liberal democracies generally, for judiciaries, by virtue of their activities in making judgments about the constitutionality of legislation, to constrain other branches of government; to be increasingly willing to do so, and therefore to become increasingly drawn into partisan political conflicts. Of course, this was nothing new in the Italian case. The 'Tangentopoli' scandal and Berlusconi had drawn the judiciary into partisan conflict long ago. Before that, a growing willingness of judges to go beyond acting as *bouches de la loi* (Guarnieri, 1997: 158) had seen them, as we mentioned earlier in the volume, taking penal initiatives in areas such as workplace safety to act as problem solvers, attempting to tackle the great social issues of the day (Newell, 2005). And before that, the establishment of the Constitutional Court in 1956—combined with the fundamental rights and freedoms in Part 1 of the Constitution and the discretion afforded to individual judges to request rulings on the constitutionality of laws—meant that the ordinary and constitutional judiciary in dialogue with one another had come to acquire what was to all intents and purposes a legislative function. This was because an increasing number of the Constitutional Court's judgments came to consist of 'binding interpretations', that is, rulings to the effect that legislation was only to be considered constitutional if interpreted in certain specific ways. And as the volume of such judgments had accumulated, so they had conditioned the activities of legislators, who were increasingly obliged, in framing legislation, to anticipate the likelihood of referrals and so to engage in modes of reasoning similar to those of the Court itself.

The Court's verdict in January 2017 seemed to represent another example, if not a further extension of this trend since by ruling that certain parts of the Italicum were unconstitutional and therefore inapplicable, it in effect created a new electoral law—as was implicitly acknowledged by the media which referred to the law resulting from the Court's judgment as the 'Legalicum' (following a 2014 judgment concerning the 2005 electoral law whose partial unconstitutionality was said to have given rise to the 'Consultellum', a word reflecting the by then well-established tradition of using 'Latin' portmanteaus to refer to electoral laws).

The Court's verdict retained the majority premium but abolished the run-off ballot. The provision allowing party leaders to occupy the first place on their lists of candidates in up to 10 electoral colleges was retained. However, they would no longer be able to decide which of the colleges to represent in the event that they were elected in more than one of them (which in future would be decided by drawing lots) since this allowed them more or less to determine which of the candidates placed after them actually got elected. It thus undermined Article 48 of the Constitution which stipulates that votes must be 'personal and equal, free and secret'. And since the constitutional reform proposals at stake in the 2016 referendum had been rejected, meaning that the Senato della Repubblica (Senate of the Republic) would retain its existing powers, it was a matter of consensus among politicians and informed political commentators that before there could be fresh elections, the Italicum as amended by the Constitutional Court would have to be reformed, or else extended to the Senate.

The issue was whether—and if so how soon—the parties would be able to overcome their interlocking vetoes in order to bring about such a result. While agreement was eventually reached—reflecting an unusual degree of cross-party consensus—on a reform which would introduce a list-based system of proportional representation, the accord collapsed following a secret parliamentary vote on 8 June 2017. The way parliamentarians vote is usually a matter of public record but in the Camera dei Deputati (Chamber of Deputies) a secret vote can be requested for matters concerning the electoral law. Secret votes make it possible for disaffected minorities within parties to sabotage legislative proposals and this is what happened in the present case, making it clear that the agreement reached by the leaders of the four main parties, the Partito Democratico (PD—Democratic Party), the MoViemento 5 Stelle (M5S—Five Star Movement), Forza Italia (FI—Forza Italia (Forward Italy, or Come on Italy!) and the Lega Nord (LN—Northern League), was not capable of actually being delivered. Consequently, it was not until 26 October, just four months before the end of the legislature, that a formula capable of mobilizing a parliamentary majority behind it could be found. The Rosato Law, or Rosatellum (after the name of its principal sponsor) was passed with the support of the PD, FI, the League, Alternativa Popolare (AP—Popular Alternative[3]) and various minor formations—but with the implacable opposition of the M5S, Articolo UNO—Movimento Democratico e Progressista (MDP—Democratic and Progressive Movement) and Sinistra Italiana (SI—Italian Left).

The Rosatellum envisaged the country being divided into 232 single-member constituencies for the Chamber of Deputies (102 for the Senate), the remaining 386 seats (207 in the case of the Senate) being elected through multi-member constituencies in which parties and coalitions of parties would present closed lists. Each multi-member constituency would thus be associated with two or more single-member constituencies. The voter would be given a ballot paper showing the names of her single-member candidates beneath each of which would appear the symbols of the supporting party or parties together with the names of their multi-member candidates. The voter would be able to express a single vote, either for his chosen party, in which case the vote would also count in favour of the single-member candidate supported by the party, or else for the single-member candidate. Such votes would be automatically distributed among the supporting parties, in proportion to their total vote in the relevant constituency, and so also count for the purposes of assigning the multi-member seats. The single-member scats would be distributed according to the simple plurality formula, the remaining seats proportionally. National thresholds of 10% and 3% were set, respectively, for coalitions (lists having received less than 1% nationally were not included in this total) and single-party lists.

As such, the Rosatellum was passed with the support of the centre-right because it met the needs of the bloc's various components which, leaving aside the minor parties, had, by the time of the law's passage, essentially become three in number.

The first of these was the League. In the aftermath of the 2012 party funding scandal and its poor performance at the 2013 election, at the end of that year the LN had come under the leadership of the 40-year-old Matteo Salvini who had developed a completely new strategy for his party by drawing upon the dramatic decline in public confidence in the European Union (EU). This had come about thanks, first, to growing awareness of the restrictions placed by membership of the eurozone on the Government's room for economic manoeuvre—restrictions exacerbated by a public debt which in 2014 stood at 134% of gross domestic product (GDP)—in attempting to deal with the consequences of years of low growth, and second, to the role of the refugee crisis in exposing the conflict between the Schengen Area free movement arrangements, and the 'Dublin principle'. Placing responsibility for assessing asylum claims on the government of the first country of arrival (and so enabling other states to reject claims and send migrants back to Italy), 'Dublin' had created tensions between the Italian Government and the EU over the demand for common EU crisis management. Salvini therefore saw an opportunity for his party to break out of the ghetto it was in—as a regional autonomy party directing anti-establishment protest against the central authorities in Rome—by becoming an anti-immigrant, nationalist party directing anti-establishment sentiment against Brussels. Thus, at the 2014 elections to the European Parliament, the party had adopted the slogan, 'Basta Euro!' ('Stop the Euro!'), and during the course of 2017 dropped the word 'North' from its title enabling it, in 2018, to field candidates throughout the country.

The second was FdI, which had emerged in December 2012 when a number of Popolo della Libertà (PdL—People of Freedom) spokespersons broke with the party, allegedly with Berlusconi's agreement, in order to create a formation that would appeal specifically to that variety of right-wing sentiment according to which being on the right meant having socially conservative attitudes and an affinity with the ideals of national pride never entirely relinquished by the heirs of Mussolini.

Finally, the third component, FI, projected an image that was inevitably inseparable from that of Berlusconi himself. Once the principal representative of Italian populism, the now elderly Berlusconi had turned his back on his flamboyant past, aware that the 'anti-establishment' mantle had been taken over by other parties. He therefore sought to create distinctiveness for his party by projecting the image of the wise elder statesman able to appeal to moderate voters who might otherwise have been dissuaded from voting for the centre-right either because of the stridency of the League or the hints of neo-fascism in the narratives of FdI.

Thus, for the election in 2018, the parties of the centre-right needed both to project unity—so that together they could pose as a credible governing coalition and seek an overall majority on that basis—and to maintain the visibility of their distinctive profiles to enable them to appeal effectively to their distinctive constituencies. The requirement for visibility was particularly important to Salvini whose party now rivalled FI in opinion polls and who could expect successfully to challenge Berlusconi for leadership of the centre-right as a whole if his party could overtake that of the entrepreneur. The new electoral law satisfied the double requirement perfectly. On the one hand, in requiring a combined list of the centre-right, the Italicum as amended in January 2017 would have disadvantaged the component parties thanks to the fact that their voters were not, as we saw earlier, easily summable. On the other hand, a purely proportional system would have accentuated the differences between them to a degree that might have been equally damaging. With the new electoral law the parties got the best of both worlds as they could present their own lists and agree on candidates to be presented in the single-member constituencies with all votes for the lists counting in favour of the single-member candidates.

The PD, for its part, appears to have calculated that the law would disincentivize defections to its left, a possibility whose likelihood seemed to be heightened by the emergence of two new groups, SI and MDP. These had come into being in February, partly as a result of the departure from the PD of certain of its representatives who disagreed with Renzi on the fundamental question of the kind of centre-left party they wanted to build and were joined, in varying proportions, by members of SEL. If the two groups added to the now rather numerous array of parties and movements to the left of the PD, then in the run-up to the 2018 elections three of them (MDP, Possibile and SI) together formed a new alliance, Liberi e Uguali (LeU—Free and Equal), led by the President of the Senate, Pietro Grasso, while the two communist parties set about running together as Potere al Popolo (PaP—Power to the People)—neither with any real electoral success, since LeU won only 3.4% of the vote and the election of 14 deputies, while PaP took 1.1% but won no seats.

The PD also calculated that the new law would create difficulties for the M5S. This party, it was thought, would struggle to make headway, first, because its candidates in the single-member constituencies would be obliged to seek votes on two fronts, both the right and the left, and second because, to a degree greater than the other parties, the M5S lacked potential candidates with sufficient notoriety locally to enable them to benefit from personal appeals in the single-member constituencies. Finally, the PD calculated that in the absence of a majority for any of the contenders, it would at least be able, through a mainstream coalition with FI, to exclude the populists, the League and the M5S, from office.

In dissolving the Parlamento (Parliament) on 28 December 2017, the President fired the starting gun on a campaign in which the immigration issue had a very high profile. This was especially true given the events of 3 February when a 28-year-old, Luca Traini, with evident far-right sympathies, went on the rampage in the city of Macerata, wounding with a shotgun six people, all of whom were of sub-Saharan African origin. Both the League and the M5S, among others, exploited the event to frame immigration as a significant problem. While condemning violence, Matteo Salvini declared that the incident was evidence that what he called 'uncontrolled immigration' led to social conflict. The Movement's Alessandro di Battista, meanwhile, responded to condemnation by spokespersons for the mainstream parties by demanding silence on the part of those who had 'political responsibilities' for what had happened.

If the salience of the immigration issue benefited the League, then FI in contrast retreated because Berlusconi, as a one-time populist protester-turned-moderate, suffered from a loss of votes on two fronts—of protesters to the League and of both protesters and moderates to the M5S; for the latter ran a highly professional campaign in which it was successful in portraying itself, simultaneously, both as a party of anti-establishment protest (personified by the Third World activist and outgoing M5S deputy, Alessandro Di Battista, who significantly had a frontline role but was not actually a candidate) and as a party of government (personified by its youthful prime ministerial candidate, Luigi di Maio, who constantly emphasized the Movement's governing credentials by always appearing in a shirt and tie). In this way it was able to mobilize those driven by the long-standing and deep-seated anti-political sentiments of Italian voters; those driven mainly by disappointment with the outgoing Government, and those who might otherwise have been attracted by the new-found moderate profile of an 81-year-old Berlusconi who was once an anti-establishment figure but who, having had several turns at the helm, no longer convinced.

The PD, meanwhile, suffered in at least three respects. Its attempts to present itself as a party with a broadly liberal social agenda—symbolized by its 'primary' elections, and their opportunities for popular participation in defining the political agenda, or its legislation on civil partnerships—meant that it was vulnerable to losses of support to a movement with a rather similar offer. Its failure to challenge assumptions that migration was a security issue and had to be put a stop to, reinforced them, thereby making it more difficult to resist the advance of the League which by then had established clear ownership of the issue. Finally, although the PD went into the election campaign with a governing record that it could credibly claim was at least satisfactory given the economic and social circumstances it had found itself having to deal with, the person who most personified these results—the outgoing Prime Minister, Paolo Gentiloni—was not his party's leader and was therefore unable to translate his personal approval ratings, which were rather good, into support for the PD as such.

As is so often the case in Italian politics, the election outcome (see Table 7.1) seemed to represent a watershed. From the point of view of the party system and the distribution of the vote, it was in many respects similar to that of the election held five years previously. The principal forces in contention—the centre-right, the centre-left and the M5S—remained the same; and although the relative strengths of the three aggregations changed significantly—with the centre-left shifting from first to third place, the centre-right from second to first and the M5S from third to second—the party system retained the tripolar format that had emerged in 2013. Thus, as was the case pre-viously, essentially the country was divided between three blocks none of which commanded an overall majority or would willingly enter into coalition with either of the others. The two great winners were the M5S (which increased its share of the vote from 25.6% to 32.7%) and the League (up from 4.1% to 17.3%), while the two great losers were the PD (down from 25.4% to 18.7%) and FI (which garnered 13.9% of the vote compared with the 21.6% the PdL had taken in 2013); the outcome confirmed for a second time that neither of the political logics—consensual or majoritarian—according to which government formation had taken place until 2013 was available any longer.

In the immediate aftermath of the vote few, even among informed commentators, were willing to predict what the composition of the new government would be. On the one hand, it appeared that the M5S would have to form the mainstay of the incoming government; for, as the largest party but without a majority it was too small to govern alone but too strong to be excluded: there was no majority for a 'mainstream' FI-PD coalition. The parties of the centre-right did not command a majority either. On the other hand, they constituted the largest single coalition represented in Parliament, and the League's Matteo Salvini had explicitly ruled out a governing arrangement with the M5S—which seemed understandable. Berlusconi now appeared to be a spent force, so Salvini seemed likely to want to inherit his support so as to consolidate his leadership of the centre-right, and not waste such an opportunity by playing second fiddle to a government led by Di Maio. If that made everything depend on how the PD reacted to its defeat, then Renzi's post-election declaration that the party would return to opposition, made it difficult to see how any kind of governing coalition—formal or informal—could be assembled at all. Although there were one or two discordant voices among PD spokespersons, they were all aware that a governing role would mean propping up either a government of the centre-right, or a M5S government led by Di Maio—with all the risks for what remained of the PD's popularity that such a decision would entail.

In the end, the League and the M5S were able to come together thanks to a series of concessions on each side. The M5S would not govern with any coalition that included Berlusconi, thanks to his con-flict of interests and his legal difficulties, and to the amount of electoral capital the M5S had invested in its claim to be a 'clean' party whose priority was to sweep away the corruption of the old political estab-lishment. It was able to persuade the League to join it in government, without Berlusconi, on the basis of a negotiated 'contract for a

Table 7.1 Results of the 2018 Italian general election, Chamber of Deputies

Lists and coalitions	Votes		Seats			
	No.	%	Proportional arena	Majoritarian arena	Abroad	Total
Lega	5,705,925	17.3	73	50	2	125
Forza Italia	4,586,672	13.9	59	43	1	103
Fratelli d'Italia	1,440,107	4.4	19	13	–	32
Noi con l'Italia-Unione di Centro	431,042	1.3	0	5	0	5
Other centre-right	5,533	0.0	–	0	–	0
Total centre-right	*12,169,279*	*37.0*	*151*	*111*	*3*	*265*
MoVimento 5 Stelle	10,748,372	32.7	133	93	1	227
Partito Democratico	6,153,081	18.7	86	21	5	112
+Europa	845,406	2.6	0	2	1	3
Insieme	191,489	0.6	0	1	–	1
Civica Popolare	180,539	0.5	0	2	0	2
Other centre-left	149,042	0.4	2	2	–	4
Total centre-left	*7,519,557*	*22.9*	*88*	*28*	*6*	*122*
Liberi e Uguali	1,114,298	3.4	14	0	0	14
Others	1,354,919	4.1	0	0	2	2
Total	32,906,425	100	386	232	12	630

Source: based on data from Chiaramonte and Paparo (2019, Table 11.3).

government of change', the substance of which would, publicly at least, be agreed between the two parties prior to any discussion of the distribution of government portfolios. If this enabled the M5S to retain at least the semblance of continuing adherence to its principled rejection of involvement with other political forces, then it enabled the League to avoid the appearance of propping up a government led by the M5S; for, once the contract had been agreed and published the parties announced that the premiership would be assumed by neither of them but by the independent law professor, the 53-year-old Giuseppe Conte. Without a political following of his own, Conte's role would inevitably be confined to that of mediator and executor of a programme agreed by others, i.e. by the two parties whose independent profiles and capacities for mobilization of support would be assured by their occupation of the ministries most directly related to their key campaign pledges—the Ministry of the Interior in the case of Salvini, and the Ministry of Labour in the case of Di Maio.

Shortly before the new Government took office, the country seemed, briefly, to be headed for a constitutional crisis when at the end of May 2018 the President—in accordance with Article 92 of the Constitution which gives him the power to appoint government ministers on the advice of the incoming Prime Minister—refused to agree to have the Eurosceptical economist, Paolo Savona, as Minister of Finance. As Savona was strongly backed by the two Eurosceptical parties which by then had agreed to form a government and which commanded a parliamentary majority, they denounced Sergio Mattarella's decision as unconstitutional. The M5S actually threatened to impeach the President and support the League in taking its protest onto the streets.

Their positions were mistaken since Mattarella's power to appoint implied a power not to appoint and there were precedents. However, more fundamentally they were mistaken because they were based on the typical populist assumption that democratic legitimacy is merely about the supremacy, regardless, of the will of a majority, whereas it is in fact about the exercise of popular sovereignty 'in the forms and within the limits of the Constitution' (as Article 1 puts it clearly).

On the other hand, Mattarella's move was condemned as politically unwise as it initially seemed, in the face of the parties' resistance, that it could only lead to fresh elections after which the League and the M5S, which had already spooked the markets, were likely to come back even stronger. This position too was mistaken. Had Mattarella given way to pressure from the parties he would have set a constitutional precedent, bequeathing a weakened presidency to his successors. Ultimately, he successfully called the parties' bluff: neither was willing to accept the risks associated with fresh elections so soon after the last ones, and thus they shifted Savona to the lesser role of Minister of European Affairs.

The prospects for the new Government seemed highly uncertain. On the one hand, it had a secure seat majority in the Chamber of Deputies (although a slightly less secure majority in the Senate), and according to opinion polls published shortly after it took office, the Government enjoyed the support of about 57% of those expressing a party preference. On the other hand, there were significant potential threats to its cohesion. Conte was ill-placed to act as an authoritative leader. Although the two governing parties had been thrown together by their populism, there were significant differences in their electoral and ideological profiles. The League had its electoral centre of gravity among small business people in the prosperous north and was sustained by popular fears surrounding immigration, while the M5S had its centre of gravity in the poorer south and drew its support from across the left-right spectrum including some on the radical/libertarian left.

There were several other sources of instability. One was the migrant crisis, which maintained a high profile throughout 2018 and on into 2019 thanks to a range of initiatives introduced by Salvini as Minister of the Interior, including closing Italian ports to migrant rescue vessels; isolating non-governmental organizations involved in Mediterranean search and rescue operations; and adopting a more aggressive stance in EU negotiations on the issue—which did little, practically, to resolve the underlying humanitarian emergency but provided a convenient platform from which to capitalize on popular prejudices, even though the number of arrivals had declined dramatically since the 2017 agreement with the Libyan Government. Clearly a source of strength for the League, the issue was troublesome for a party like the M5S whose populism was of the 'inclusionary' rather than the 'exclusionary' variety; which had to a degree wanted to speak up for immigrants as one component of its broad conception of 'the people' whose interests were being trampled on by a privileged elite; which attracted support from disillusioned left-wing voters, and which therefore stood to lose as much as to gain from associating itself with the chauvinist rhetoric of Salvini.

A second source of instability lay in the parties' need to deliver on their election pledges to their core constituencies: the single rate of income tax (dubbed the 'flat tax') in the case of the League; the citizenship income in the case of the M5S. These pledges seemed bound to divide the parties as they were fundamentally incompatible. This was because both implied considerable increases in deficit spending in the context of severe financial and economic constraints deriving from the EU's Fiscal Compact and years of sluggish growth, and because if each appealed by and large to the supporters of the party promoting it, then it was much less attractive to the supporters of the other party, located, as they were, in distinct parts of the country.

While the flagship measures both informed the budgetary process in 2018—along with a reform of the pensions system known as the 'quota 100' (providing a right to retire once the sum of the retiree's age and the years for which he or she had contributed amounted to 100)—and led to the predictable tussles with the European Commission later in the year, ultimately, a compromise was reached. With the 2019 European Parliament elections in the offing, neither the Commission nor other EU member states wanted to provide the Italian Government with the basis for an anti-EU campaign, while the Italian Government was not prepared to risk a financial crisis in the run-up to the elections. Thus, having been threatened with the EU's Excessive Deficit Procedure in November, the following month the Government agreed to a general government deficit target of 2.04% of GDP in place of the 2.4% it had wanted, along with safeguard clauses to narrow the gap in subsequent years. Essentially, these clauses involved legislating for future value-added tax rises—to prevent deficits from expanding in the event that growth projections failed to materialize—with the evident risk that, in a practice inherited from previous governments, they would, when the time came, merely be decommissioned to be replaced with larger increases pencilled in for a time even further into the future.

Finally, in early and mid-2019 a number of issues began to create tension between the two parties because they lay at the core of their identities and claims to office: one was the proposed high-speed rail link known as the Treno ad Alta Velocità (high-speed train) between Turin and Lyon in France, which went to the heart of the movement's sustainability agenda but was strongly supported by the League; another involved allegations of corruption against League spokespersons in April and July, which were central to the movement's 'clean government' agenda.

In mid-2019, one year on from the formation of the Government, its prospects seemed no less certain than they had when it had taken office. Overall, it remained popular, continuing to enjoy essentially the same level of support in voting intention polls as it had done earlier. However, the overall figure masked a significant change in the relative strength of the two parties as was confirmed by the results of the European Parliament elections in May when the League took an astonishing, although not unexpected, 34.3% of the vote (double its 2018 vote share) and the M5S took 17.1% (representing a little over half what it had enjoyed in 2018). The PD, meanwhile, recovered slightly by taking 22.7% of the vote, thereby regaining some of the ground it had lost since 2013. The 'establishment'-'anti-establishment', or 'populist'-'mainstream' divide in Italian politics seemed to have become superimposed on the traditional left-right cleavage. On the one hand, the League made significant inroads into the support previously enjoyed by the M5S and FI to consolidate its leadership of the forces of the (centre-)right; while on the centre-left, the PD, though winning back little of the support it had lost to the M5S a year earlier, was more successful than the latter in getting its supporters actually to turn out, thus enabling it to displace the M5S as the political system's second largest party.

Thus, in mid-2019 Italy was governed by two parties which had in common their populism, but which seemed to be finding it increasingly difficult to live with each other because they represented different varieties of populism with different priorities—one representing a reaction to the erosion of traditional social values and customs, the other a reaction to a perceived lack of responsiveness of the political system in a context of economic distress.

Matters came to a head in August 2019 when, seeking to capitalize on his party's considerable lead in the opinion polls, Salvini declared that the M5S was standing in the way of a series of essential reforms and that he wanted fresh elections. Events moved quickly. Conte, whose authority had clearly been challenged, refused to resign, demanding, in the interests of transparency, that the political crisis first be debated in Parliament—to which the League responded with the threat of a motion of no confidence in the Government. In his address to Parliament, on 20 August, Conte defended his Government's record and accused the League of disloyalty—before announcing that he would tender his resignation to the President of the Republic in whom responsibility for managing the crisis would from then on inevitably reside. Salvini's bluff had been called, and in the days that followed, he made several attempts to row back from a threat which polls suggested might be less profitable than he had anticipated, while the President undertook the obligatory series of consultations with the political parties to establish whether some new governing majority could be formed in the interests of avoiding having to dissolve Parliament at a critical juncture internationally and so soon after the previous dissolution.

All eyes then focused on negotiations for the formation of a new government between the M5S and the PD. On the one hand, the M5S was aware that it was caught on the horns of a dilemma consisting of a choice between fresh elections that seemed likely to see it retreat before an advancing hard right, or else agreeing to be part of a new government with the risk that its formation would be perceived as being the result of elite-level skulduggery and so undermine the credibility of its central claim: that its autonomy and anti-establishment profile made it uniquely qualified to represent the interests of ordinary Italians against those of political and economic elites. The PD, on the other hand, faced a dilemma that was the mirror-image of the one facing the M5S, aware that avoiding elections and the possible advance of the right would require it to govern with a party whose reliability seemed doubtful precisely because its inclusionary populism led it to look for support in two opposite directions: to the centre left as far as the inclusionary element was concerned, but to Salvini's right when it came to the populist element.

Ultimately, the desire of both parties to obstruct the advance of the right in the immediate term and thus avoid the political upheavals that seemed likely to flow from that, won the day. On 29 August 2019 Conte received a presidential mandate for the formation of a government; on 5 September the new 'yellow-red' Government was sworn in; on 9 and 10 September respectively, it won the confirmatory votes of confidence in the Chamber of Deputies and Senate, respectively. The outcome contained a certain irony in that the PD spokesperson who did most to rally his party behind it was its former leader, Matteo Renzi, who in the immediate aftermath of the 2018 elections had explicitly vetoed an agreement with the M5S. This apparent volte face was in all probability to be explained by the commonalities between Renzi and M5S leader, Luigi Di Maio. Both inhabited a 'post-ideological' world. If for Di Maio the terms 'left' and 'right' no longer had meaning and what counted was merely 'solutions', then Renzi, as we saw in the previous chapter, had made pragmatism—the construction of whatever tactical alliances were necessary to solve immediate-term problems—one of the trademarks of his approach to 'doing' politics. Thus, for Renzi and his followers, the outcome was not just a necessity: it contained possibilities.

The PD had in March 2019 elected a new secretary: the Lazio regional president, Nicola Zingaretti. Following an interim period while elections could be arranged, he had taken over the leadership after Matteo Renzi had finally been obliged to resign thanks to the party's electoral setback the previous year. For Zingaretti, the formation of the new Government carried the risk of a growth in perceptions that it was the work of a party elite that continued to lack a narrative that large swathes of the population could identify with; whose grassroots organizations were continuing to weaken, and which had no clear answers to the popular anger and frustration that fed the exclusionary populism it was trying to keep at bay.

At the end of 2019, therefore, the impression was of an Italian polity under siege, of a Government struggling, in the face of an advancing hard right, to retain its hold on office. On the one hand, the incumbent Government was an active one. The programmatic statement on the basis of which Conte had asked Parliament, in September, to pass the usual confirmatory motion of confidence had contained at least 21 specific commitments, promising legislative action to, among other things, raise the school-leaving age; end offshore drilling; introduce a minimum wage; ensure equal pay for men and women; reduce the number of accidents at work; and increase the efficiency of the judicial system. By the end of November, of the 21 commitments, there seemed to be evidence of action on at least 11 of them; and the impression of an unusually active Government was confirmed by OpenPolis data[4] which showed that with three decree laws passed per month, the Government could claim to be more active than any of the six that had preceded it, and therefore the most active in the past 10 years. On the other hand, active policymaking had made little impression on the poll numbers. On 27 October regional elections in Umbria, traditionally part of the country's central 'red belt', had seen the right's candidate for regional president romp home, outdistancing by over 20 percentage points the candidate, Vincenzo Bianconi, who the PD and the M5S had decided to field jointly. The M5S itself had scored a miserable 7.4% as its time in government had rendered it increasingly 'establishment-looking' and deprived it of the capacity to mobilize the protest vote, now more or less monopolized by Salvini. Lacking a clear ideological profile or much by way of a presence on the ground, and divided between *sovranisti* (sovereignists), *filo-europei* (Europhiles) and *movimentisti* (supporters of grassroots initiatives), the M5S appeared to be imploding. Not surprisingly, the outcome led Di Maio to attempt to regain some political initiative by calling for a review of the coalition agreement with the PD (*Today*, 2019), and few were willing to bet much on the Government surviving long into the New Year.

If that meant that the task for the PD in seeking to contain an advancing right was to win over former M5S voters, then it appeared difficult in the extreme. Already at the time of the European elections it was clear that 2018 M5S voters shifting to the centre-left were a very small minority as compared to those who abandoned the movement by abstaining (Istituto Cattaneo, 2019), and it was clear again at the regional elections in Umbria (CISE, 2019). Only about 25% of M5S voters located themselves on the left of the political spectrum, and on most issues even they were closer to the League than to the PD (De Sio and Angelucci, 2019).

Against this background, the emergence, towards the end of 2019, of the Sardine—a spontaneous movement of protest against processes of bordering (Yuval-Davis *et al.* 2019) and against the populist right, its political language and assumptions—testified to the sheer weakness of parties of the left in facing the hard-right tide. It was as if the parties within the representative institutions of government, unable to provide the necessary leadership, had seen their role as the main protagonists of resistance to the onslaught taken over by a new social movement. There seemed little doubt that the Sardine played a crucial, possibly decisive, role in helping the PD to see off the League's challenge in the 26 January regional election in Emilia-Romagna, which lay at the heart of the traditional 'red belt', or that this shortened the odds on the Government's survival at least marginally. Few at the time were aware that the odds on the Government's survival were about to shorten further—this time rather markedly.

Notes

1 After the building in which it is housed.
2 For example, one concerned the provision for voters to choose a party and its 'head-of-list' candidate (who could run in up to 10 constituencies, other candidates being confined to a single constituency) and to cast two additional preference votes for candidates of his/her chosen party. Since small parties were far less likely than larger parties to be able to elect any but their 'head-of-list' candidates, the Coordinating Group for Constitutional Democracy held the provision to be incompatible with Article 51 of the Constitution, according to which citizens are 'eligible for public and elected offices on equal terms'. However, there were several other grounds on which the cases were brought.
3 This was the name the NCD chose for itself in March 2017 as part of an attempt to pursue an alliance with FI to the exclusion of the League and Fratelli d'Italia (FdI—Brothers of Italy) considered as being positioned too far to the right.
4 See www.openpolis.it/numeri/il-governo-conte-ii-con-una-media-di-3-decreti-legge-al-mese/.

8   Conclusion

Historically, Italian domestic politics have been more significantly affected by events going on beyond the border of the polity than is true for many if not most other liberal democracies. In the aftermath of the Second World War, the nature of the party system was profoundly shaped by the Cold War. However, the unusual degree of influence of the international environment is, arguably, one that can be traced back to the very beginnings of Italy as a unified state. Immediately after the *risorgimento* (unification), divergences between north and south which had previously never been perceived as a 'problem' or a 'question' as such were suddenly conceptualized as a relationship of superiority/inferiority precisely because of their implications for capitalist industrialization and perceptions of the new state's position on the international stage. Italian political elites' anxieties about their state's standing in the world have been a constant of Italian political history, so much so that they have become part of the political culture. The citizens of most countries regard themselves as anomalous or exceptional in some ways. The French talk about *l'exception française*; nationalist discourse in Britain suggests that there is something special with British development; the term 'American exceptionalism' is widely used in that country; in Germany, historians talk about the *Sonderweg* or 'special path'. However, in all these cases, exceptionalism is seen as having a positive valence, whereas in the Italian case, it is viewed negatively, as evidence that the country is, in some not very clear sense, not normal.

> Thus Massimo D'Alema ... wrote a book in 1995 called *Un paese normale*, his ambition for Italy; a collection of essays by the late Enzo Biagi recently published by Rizzoli was given the title of *Consigli per un paese normale*; on 4 August 2010 Dario Franceschini, former leader of the ... Democratic Party declared in the Chamber of Deputies '*Non viviamo in un paese normale*'.
>
> (Sassoon, 2013)

In the aftermath of the Second World War, the breath-taking indifference to principles of non-interference with which American governments intervened in Italian domestic politics led Italians to refer to their country as *un paese a sovranità limitata* (a country of limited sovereignty), a state of affairs that was accepted with a mixture of resignation (it enabled the country to shelter under the US nuclear umbrella) and resentment (as it emphasized the country's subordination on the international stage). Meanwhile, the Cold War divide prevented the main political parties, the Democrazia Cristiana (DC—Christian Democrats) and the Partito Comunista Italiano (PCI—Italian Communist Party), from acting as effective agents of national integration, for it helped to perpetuate a situation in which each party had a vision of 'the good society' in which the world view of the other could find no place. Although both parties were committed to democracy and to making the 1948 Constitution work, neither of them drew inspiration from unification, their main communities of reference lying, rather, outside the country: the international working class for the PCI; the worldwide Catholic Church for the DC (Newell, 2010a: 151). If the anti-fascism of the parties responsible for drafting the Constitution was the founding ideology of the Republic and provided some basis for national cohesion, then it could never be complete as it inevitably excluded the *nostalgici* who became *esuli in patria*, or exiles in their own country (Tarchi, 1995). Consequently, citizens' primary loyalties were party political rather than national, and public displays of patriotism were things which, thanks to the painful memories of 1943, Italians tended to avoid.

Since the ending of the Cold War, developments on the international stage have been no less important for understanding the unfolding of Italian domestic politics, indeed arguably more so as European integration and the processes of globalization have gathered pace. If, prior to the 1990s, European integration had not proceeded far enough for it to figure highly in Italy's domestic politics, now it has arguably not gone far enough to prevent it from doing so. As fiscal integration has lagged behind monetary integration, the pooling of sovereignty has prevented the development of 'fiscal solidarity' between the 'weaker' and the 'stronger' parts, thus placing severe strains on the management of crisis situations, and so heightening perceptions in countries like Italy that their destinies are in the hands of authorities over which they can exercise little effective control. Meanwhile, the population movements arising from war, climate change and new social networks have affected Italy more than most European Union member states because it is a country with an external EU border.

As the world becomes increasingly integrated, so too will Italian domestic politics increasingly reflect processes of development and change extending well beyond Italy—processes of development and change affecting the 'supply' and the 'demand' sides of politics in ways that have become increasingly evident since at least the ending of the Cold War. With that event, which seemed to mark 'the end of history', mainstream parties of the left began to lose whatever remained of the cultural hegemony (as expressed in the United Kingdom, for instance, by the so-called social democratic consensus) they had acquired in the aftermath of the Second World War. From the end of the Cold War on, unbridled capitalism and the neo-liberal consensus were 'the only games in town'. The declining significance of traditional social divisions, of religion and class, in bringing with it a decline in the extent to which voting choices were influenced by hereditary and prescriptive ties, led to more sceptical, more volatile voters. The declining significance of the traditional 'mass' parties, along with the mediatization and the personalization of politics, was accompanied by declining levels of political engagement and the growth of 'audience democracy' (Manin, 1997), with voters increasingly cast in the role of passive spectators of the 'political spectacle'. Finally, globalization and the emergence of supranational institutions led to a draining away of power from national legislatures and an emerging gap between the 'haves'—the well educated in secure, well-paid employment, comfortable with the cultural changes effected by globalization—and the 'have-nots'—the less-well educated, whose jobs are rendered insecure by the increasing international mobility of capital and who are uncomfortable with the cultural changes, such as those associated with mass migration, that globalization has brought with it. Unable to discern significant differences between the mainstream parties of the left and right—which in turn are restricted, by globalization, in terms of the differences they can offer—it is the 'have-nots' who have formed the principal audience for the populist 'political entrepreneurs', of whose emergence and growth the recent successes of the MoVimento 5 Stelle and the Lega (League) represent the Italian expression.

Populism is a dangerous and potentially anti-democratic phenomenon because in claiming to be the only authentic representatives of the interests of the people in opposition to those of outsiders and elites, populist leaders suggest, implicitly, that others are illegitimate as contenders for office and that majority backing entitles them to ignore constitutional constraints and minority guarantees. Their claims to have the solution to problems others have been unable to resolve if only they are put in charge, leads them to deny the complexities of modern politics and to raise expectations to a degree that can only result in disappointment.

In early 2020 right-wing populism in Italy, notwithstanding the continuation of some nasty episodes, such as those surrounding Silvia Romano,[1] seemed to be losing some of its force. Support for the League had fallen below 30%; polling pointed to a decline in popular hostility and resentment towards migrants.[2] Patriotism is always ambiguous. In the hands of the right it tends to mean the exclusion of others; in the hands of the left it means a sense of community, inclusion and solidarity in the service of a common purpose. As Italy sought to cope with COVID-19, there was an evident sense of patriotism in the latter sense and the country seemed less anxious about itself. Italians suddenly became aware that they had a health service that was second to none and that they were, on the whole, coping much better with the pandemic than many if not most other countries including many among their European neighbours. They had something to feel very proud of. With a deep recession in the offing and levels of public debt set to exceed 150% of gross domestic product in the coming months it was obvious that there were extremely tough times ahead. But perhaps they would also be happier ones as well.

Guide to further reading

There is a wealth of material on contemporary Italian politics in English. Assuming that the typical reader of this volume is one who is approaching the subject matter for the first time and wants guidance on where to go next, then he or she could do worse than to begin with the most engaging general history of Italian politics and society from 1943 (up until the 1980s) that I know of: Paul Ginsborg's *A History of Contemporary Italy, Society and Politics 1943–1988* published in 1990, by Penguin. After that he or she could progress to the series of 'Politics in Italy' volumes which, with the sponsorship of the Istituto Cattaneo in Bologna, have been published each year since 1986. Each provides discussion and analysis of the relevant year's most significant political and social events and changes. The series has been in the hands of various publishers over time. From 2000 it was published by Berghahn; since 2018 it has appeared each year as a special issue of the journal, *Contemporary Italian Politics*. Readers wanting political science explanations of the current structures and functioning of the institutions of Italian governance and policymaking could consult my *Politics in Italy: Governance in a Normal Country* (Cambridge University Press,

2010). Gianfranco Pasquino has recently published a more up-to-date text: *Italian Democracy: How it Works* (Routledge, 2019).

Notes

1 Silvia Romano was the 24-year-old aid worker who had been kidnapped and held for 18 months while working in Africa, and who returned to Italy on 10 May 2020. During her captivity she had apparently converted to Islam and there was speculation, on her return to Italy, that the Government had paid a ransom in order to secure her release. After her return she was subject to a deluge of hate messages on social media including a speech in Parliament by the League deputy, Alessandro Pagano, who referred to her as a 'neo-terrorist'.
2 As the pandemic of coronavirus disease (COVID-19) spread, and frontiers were closed, it became apparent that a significant labour shortage was developing in the agricultural sector and that at the same time there were large numbers of foreigners, many of them failed asylum seekers, without residence permits. Consequently, while there was a demand for agricultural labour that was not being satisfied, on the other hand there were large numbers of workers unable to meet it if not through the black market dominated by organized crime gangs. Italia Viva Minister of Agriculture, Teresa Bellanova, therefore proposed the regularization of these workers, a move supported, according to an EMG poll, by a relative majority of 42% of respondents, with 37% responding negatively and 21% preferring not to answer. See https://sondaggibidimedia.com/sondaggio-emg-covid-12-5/2/.

References

Barigazzi, J. (2008) 'Miracle in 100 Days: How Berlusconi Brought Order to Chaotic Italy and What Comes Next', *Newsweek*, 9 August.

Bordignon, Fabio and Ceccarini, Luigi (2019) 'Five Stars, Five Years, Five (Broken) Taboos', in Luigi Ceccarini and James L. Newell (eds), *The Italian General Election of 2018: Italy in Uncharted Territory*, Basingstoke: Palgrave Macmillan, pp. 139–163.

Bull, Martin J. and Newell, James L. (2005) *Italian Politics: Adjustment under Duress*, Cambridge: Polity Press.

Caccavale, Michele (1997) *Il grande inganno*, Milan: Kaos edizioni.

Calise, Mauro (2000) *Il partito personale*, Rome and Bari: Laterza.

Capano, Giliberto and Giuliani, Marco (2001) 'Governing Without Surviving? An Italian Paradox: Law-Making in Italy 1987–2001', *Journal of Legislative Studies*, 4: 13–36.

Centro Italiano Studi Elettorali (CISE) (2019) 'Flussi Perugia: massiccia smobilitazione dell'elettorato M5S: che ha ceduto alla Lega più di quanto sia rimasto al Movimento', Rome: Centro Italiano Studi Elettorali, https://cise.luiss.it/cise/2019/10/28/flussi-perugia-massiccia-smobilitazione-dellelettorato-m5s-che-ha-ceduto-alla-lega-piu-di-quanto-sia-rimasto-al-movimento/.

Chabod, Federico (1961) *L'Italia Contemporanea (1918–1948)*, Turin: Einaudi.

Chiaramonte, Alessandro and Paparo, Aldo (2019) 'Volatile Voters and a Volatile Party System: The Results of the 2018 Italian General Election', in Luigi Ceccarini and James L. Newell (eds), *The Italian General Election of 2018: Italy in Uncharted Territory*, Basingstoke: Palgrave Macmillan, pp. 247–70.

Cremonesi, M. (2012) 'Via Bellerio? Era il Bancomat di Renzo', *Corriere della Sera*, 4 April, p. 6.

D'Alimonte, Roberto (2013) 'The Italian Elections of February 2013: The End of the Second Republic?', *Contemporary Italian Politics*, 5(2): 113–129.

De Sio, Lorenzo and Angelucci, Davide (2019) 'Il PD alla conquista dell'elettorato M5s: è possibile? E come?', Rome: Centro Italiano Studi Elettorali, https://cise.luiss.it/cise/2019/11/06/il-pd-alla-conquista-dell-elettorato-m5s-e-possibile-e-come/.

Emanuele, Vincenzo and Chiaramonte, Alessandro (2020) 'Going Out of the Ordinary. The De-Institutionalisation of the Italian Party System in Comparative Perspective', *Contemporary Italian Politics*, 12(1): 4–22.

European Commission (2018) *Country Report Italy 2018*, Brussels: European Commission, https://ec.europa.eu/info/sites/info/files/2018-european-semester -country-report-italy-en.pdf.

Fabbrini, S. and Lazar, M. (2013) 'Still a Difficult Democracy? Italy between Populist Challenges and Institutional Weakness', *Contemporary Italian Politics*, 5(2): 106–112.

Fiori, Giuseppe (1995) *Il venditore: Storia di Silvio Berlusconi e della Fininvest*, Milan: Garzanti.

Floridia, Antonio (2018) 'Electoral Systems and Concepts of Democracy: Electoral Reform as a Permanent Policy Issue in the Italian Political System', *Contemporary Italian Politics*, 10(2): 112–131.

Floridia, Antonio (2019) *Un partito sbagliato: Democrazia e organizzazione nel partito democratico*, Rome: Castelvecchi.

Furlong, Paul (2002) 'The Italian Political System in 2001: Radical Change and Work in Progress', in James L. Newell (ed.), *The Italian General Election of 2002: Berlusconi's Victory*, Manchester: Manchester University Press, pp. 11–28.

Geddes, Andrew and Pettrachin, Andrea (2020) 'Migration Policy and Politics: Exacerbating Paradoxes', *Contemporary Italian Politics*, 12(2): 227–242.

Gibelli, Antonio (2010) *Berlusconi passato alla storia: L'Italia nell'era della democrazia autoritaria*, Rome: Donzelli.

Ginsborg, Paul (1990) *A History of Contemporary Italy: Society and Politics 1943–1988*, Harmondsworth: Penguin.

Ginsborg, Paul (2005) *Silvio Berlusconi: Television, Power and Patrimony*, London: Verso.

Guarnieri, Carlo (1997) 'The Judiciary in the Italian Political Crisis', *West European Politics* 20(1): 157–175.

Hine, David (1981) 'Thirty Years of the Italian Republic: Governability and Constitutional Reform', *Parliamentary Affairs*, 34(1): 63–80.

Istituto Cattaneo (2019) 'Elezioni europee: I flussi di voto', Bologna: Istituto Cattaneo, www.cattaneo.org/wp-content/uploads/2019/05/Analisi-Istituto-Ca ttaneo-Elezioni-Europee-2019-Flussi-elettorali-in-cinque-città.pdf.

Katz, Richard and Mair, Peter (1993) 'The Evolution of Party Organizations in Europe: The Three Faces of Party Organization', *American Review of Politics*, 14: 593–618.

LaPalombara, Joseph (1964) *Interest Groups in Italian Politics*, Princeton, NJ: Princeton University Press.

Manin, Bernard (1997) *The Principles of Representative Government*, Cambridge: Cambridge University Press.

Mannheimer, R. (2008) 'Il PD delude il 40% dei suoi: Troppo remissivo', *Corriere della Sera*, 15 June, p. 11.

Montanari, A. (2008) 'Riforme, scontro tra Berlusconi e Pd Veltroni: No al dialogo se c'è l'immunità', *La Repubblica*, 19 July, p. 7.

Newell, James L. (2000) *Parties and Democracy in Italy*, Aldershot: Ashgate.

Newell, James L. (2005) 'Americanization and the Judicialization of Italian Politics', *Journal of Modern Italian Studies*, 10(1): 27–42.

Newell, James L. (2006) 'Characterising the Italian Parliament: Legislative Change in Longitudinal Perspective', *Journal of Legislative Studies*, 12(3–4): 386–403.

Newell, James L. (2009) '*Has 2008 Been a Watershed? The Significance of the Election for Italian Domestic Politics*', paper presented at a workshop entitled 'The Year After: Has Italy Entered a New Berlusconi Era?', University of Birmingham, 27 February.

Newell, James L. (2010a) *The Politics of Italy: Governance in a Normal Country*, Cambridge: Cambridge University Press.

Newell, James L. (2010b) 'Between a Rock and a Hard Place: The Governing Dilemmas of Rifondazione Comunista', in Jonathan Olsen, Michael Koß and Dan Hough (eds), *Left Parties in National Governments*, Basingstoke: Palgrave Macmillan, pp. 52–68.

Newell, James L. (2014) 'A Fight to the Death: The Challenge of the Five Star Movement and the Democratic Party's Reactions', in Carlo Fusaro and Amie Kreppel (eds), *Italian Politics*, vol. 29, New York: Berghahn, pp. 86–102.

Newell, James L. (2016) 'The MoVimento 5 Stelle (M5S), the PD and the Current (and Changing) State of the Party System', in Robert Kaiser and Jana Edelmann (eds), *Crisis as a Permanent Condition: The Italian Political System between Transition and Reform Resistance*, Baden-Baden: Nomos Verlagsgesellschaft, pp. 239–270.

Newell, James L. (2017) 'What Goes Round Comes Round: The Constitutional Court and the Forthcoming General Election', *Contemporary Italian Politics*, 9(1): 1–2.

Newell, James L. (2019) *Silvio Berlusconi: A Study in Failure*, Manchester: Manchester University Press.

Newell, James L. and Giovannini, Arianna (2015) 'The Election of the New President Has Strengthened Matteo Renzi's Grip over Italian Politics', London: London School of Economics European Politics and Policy, http://bit.ly/1Domi05.

Pasquino, Gianfranco (1997) 'No Longer a "Party State"? Institutions, Power and the Problem of Italian Reform', in Martin J. Bull and Martin Rhodes (eds), *Crisis and Transition in Italian Politics*, London and Portland, OR: Frank Cass.

Pasquino, Gianfranco (2003) 'The Government, the Opposition and the President of the Republic under Berlusconi', *Journal of Modern Italian Studies*, 8(4): 485–499.

Pasquino, Gianfranco and Pelizzo, Riccardo (2016) 'Qual'è il parlamento più produttivo?', *Casa della cultura*, www.casadellacultura.it/431/qual-e-il-parlamento-piu-produttivo-.

Pedersen, Mogens N. (1979) 'The Dynamics of European Party Systems: Changing Patterns of Electoral Volatility', *European Journal of Political Research*, 7(1): 1–26.

Pepe A. and di Gennaro, C. (2009) 'Political Protest Italian Style: The Blogosphere and Mainstream Media in the Promotion and Coverage of Beppe Grillo's V-day', *First Monday*, 4(12), www.uic.edu/htbin/cgiwrap/bin/ojs/index.php/fm /article/view/2740/2406.

Putnam, Robert D. (1988) 'Diplomacy and Domestic Politics: The Logic of Two-Level Games', *International Organization*, 42(3): 427–460.

Russo, F. and Verzichelli, L. (2009) 'A Different Legislature? The Parliamentary Scene Following the 2008 Elections', in J. L. Newell (ed.), *The Italian General Election of 2008*, London and Basingstoke: Palgrave Macmillan.

Salvadori, Massimo L. (1994) *Soria d'Italia e crisi di regime*, Bologna: il Mulino.

Sassoon, Donald (2013) 'The Italian Anomaly?' *Comparative European Politics*, 11: 280–295.

Stille, Alexander (2010) *Citizen Berlusconi: Il Cavalier Miracolo*, Milan: Garzanti.

Tarchi, Marco (1995) *Esuli in patria: I fascisti nell'Italia repubblicana*, Parma: Guanda.

Today (2019) 'Elezioni Umbria, Di Maio vuole rivedere il patto col Pd: "Meglio che con la Lega, ma ci fa male lo stesso"', *Today*, 28 October, www.today.it/politica/elezioni-umbria-conseguenze.html.

Tsebelis, G. (2002) *Veto Players: How Political Institutions Work*, Princeton, NJ: Princeton University Press and Russell Sage Foundation.

Urbani, G. (2009) Interview with Aldo Cazzullo: 'Urbani: Il progetto del "nuovo" Pdl? La debolezza del Pd ci contaggia', *Corriere della Sera*, 15 January, p. 6.

Vignati, R. (2013) 'La sfida del Movimento 5 stelle', in A. Di Virgilio and C. M. Radaelli (eds), *Politica in Italia*, Bologna: il Mulino, pp. 83–99.

Viroli, Maurizio (2010) *La libertà dei servi*, Rome and Bari: Laterza.

Yuval-Davis, Nira, Wemyss, Georgie and Cassidy, Kathryn (2019), *Bordering*, Cambridge: Polity Press.

Index

For Product Safety Concerns and Information please contact our EU
representative GPSR@taylorandfrancis.com
Taylor & Francis Verlag GmbH, Kaufingerstraße 24, 80331 München, Germany